T0110237

The Dead Came Calling

Spear Books

The Dead Came Calling

Ndũcũ wa Ngũgĩ

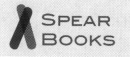

SPEAR
BOOKS

Nairobi • Kampala • Dar es Salaam • Kigali • Lusaka • Lilongwe

Published by
East African Educational Publishers Ltd.
Elgeyo Marakwet Close, off Elgeyo Marakwet Road,
Kilimani, Nairobi
P.O. Box 45314, Nairobi - 00100, KENYA
Tel: +254 20 2324760
Mobile: +254 722 205661 / 722 207216 / 733 677716 / 734 652012
Email: eaep@eastafricanpublishers.com
Website: www.eastafricanpublishers.com

East African Educational Publishers also has offices or is represented in the
following countries: Uganda, Tanzania, Rwanda, Malawi, Zambia, Botswana
and South Sudan.

© Ndūcū wa Ngūgi, 2018

All rights reserved

First published 2018

ISBN 978-9966-56-227-2

Dedication

This book is dedicated to the victims and survivors of human trafficking, and to all those fighting against this evil trade.

Acknowledgements

Thank you to my wife, Grace Gathũngũ, and our daughter, Nyambura wa Ndũcũ, for your love and words of encouragement as I toiled through writing *The Dead Came Calling*.

Thank you to my father, Ngũgĩ wa Thiong'o, for your immense support and thoughtful feedback during the writing this novel.

Thank you to my step mother, Njeri wa Ngũgĩ, my sisters, Ngĩna, Wanjikũ, Njoki, Mũmbi and brothers, Tee, Kim, Mũkoma, Bjorn, TK, for lending me your ears and your time.

Thank you to Lucas Wafula for staying the course patiently with me, to Cikũ Kĩmani-Mwanĩki for always challenging me to write more.

Thank you Wanjikũ, Beverly, James Atwater, Kĩmarũ wa Maitho, Terry Jenkins, George Mĩano, and Lynn Maloley for your friendship and support.

Chapter One

"My husband is dead."

I looked at the time: six in the morning. I sat up on my bed – legs hanging to the side, my long toes touching the floor. I rubbed the darkness from my eyes with the back of my right hand.

"Hello!" my voice crackled again, not sure what to make of this early morning intrusion.

"My husband is dead!" She repeated and broke into a sob.

Her accent told me she was Indian. It was the first call I had ever received from an Indian – any Indian, at any time – let alone so goddamn early. I pulled the phone from my ear and looked at the caller ID – restricted.

"Who is this?" I listened in again.

She continued sobbing quietly but after a few sniffles, she composed herself.

"Jack Chidi, right?" she asked.

"Yeah, who is this…?"

"Anarupa Mehta."

My mind was racing. I did not know her. How did *she* know me by name and how did she get my number?

"He is dead," she added in a near whisper.

I waited for her to elaborate but she didn't. I stood up and tagged at my underwear, which had creased up and ridden up my crotch. I turned on the light on my nightstand, an old three – legged stool, covered with a white cloth, embroidered with roses. Then I sat down again, resting my feet on the bed railing, elbows on my knees.

"Ok, I am sorry to hear about your husband, ma'am," I said. "What's his name?"

I heard her take a deep breath before she answered.

"Vishal Mehta."

I did not know any one called Vishal or even Mehta – well, except the Shekhar Mehta, a Ugandan-born Kenyan safari rally driver who had captured my imagination with his skills behind the wheel a few decades ago.

"Um, there must be a mistake," I said apologetically, shaking my head, as if she could see me.

She was quiet, for a while. Did I come across as too unfeeling? She had lost her husband after all.

"Have you called the police?" I added as if that was of any help.

"Yes, Tigoni Police."

"What did they say?"

"They're investigating – looking for clues and asking questions, I guess."

It did not make any sense – a stranger calling me to tell me that her husband was dead. She had to be confused. After all, she had already reported the matter to the police. What she needed to do now was call the office of the *Daily Grind*, where I worked as an investigative reporter, and ask them to place a death announcement in the next edition.

"Mrs. Mehta, I am not sure why you called me – but I think it's best if you just sit tight and let the police do their work."

What she said next, however, completely caught my fullest attention.

"He asked me to call you," she whispered conspiratorially.

"Who asked you to call me?"

"My husband did."

"When did he do that?" I whispered back, skeptically, for how could a dead man have asked anything.

"A few days ago," she went on. "He said should anything happen to him, I should call you."

I thought about this for a minute and then asked, "Did he tell you why?"

"He just said that you would know what to do."

She stopped and I knew she was going to start crying again.

A part of me did not want anything to do with this mystery – but she had pricked my interest nonetheless.

"What is your address?" I asked.

She told me and I hang up the phone. I looked at the time again. Seven minutes past six! It was too damn early for this.

The cigarette, dangling from my lips, sent smoke up my nostrils and into my eyes. Tears came fast and a quick rub with the back of my right hand eased the stinging pain. I put the stub out begrudgingly and threw myself back on the bed. Then I picked up my note pad. Vishal Mehta…Dead husband…Wife calls…Tigoni Police…Husband asked that she call me should anything happen to him …Why?

That was all I had – so much for note – taking.

I pulled the covers over my head and tried to catch a few winks but nothing came and I gave up. I willed myself to the shower and after I was dressed I sat down for a hurried breakfast: tea and toast as I looked over my scanty notes again. I called Bulldog, my Boss at the *Daily Grind*, to let him know that I was on my way to Tigoni – that the dead had come a – calling.

In less than ten minutes I'd caught a *matatu* to Limuru, and a short bus ride later I was walking past Tigoni Stores, an antiquated two – storied food mart, and the only concrete building standing amidst kiosks made out of tin, old kerosene and oil drums panel – beaten into rectangular submission.

It was not a long walk to get to the Mehta residence, located within a stone's throw from the exclusive Limuru Country Club where patrons enjoyed golf, tennis, swimming and the occasional horse racing. I remembered going there once as a young boy with my mother – she bet on a horse called *Luke Here*. She lost all she had – not much money but enough for us to have to walk home afterwards instead of taking a *matatu*.

The Mehta residence, a colonial mansion imposed itself on you as you walked up the cobbled driveway. To the left of it was a newer building made of brick, which seemed at odds with the Spanish architecture of the main house – but perhaps it was intended to grow on you. I knocked on the door and waited. From a distance I could hear the screams of children at a nearby primary school playing out in the fields.

The door opened. A young Indian woman ushered me in. She could not have been more than eighteen or nineteen, I thought to myself. She was wearing black jeans and a white T – shirt with Love Pink scribbled across the front. Her hair, braided into a long ponytail, whooshed across her back like a long wiper blade as she walked with a swinging gait. She had a small round Band – Aid on her nose – the kind used to pull blackheads. I wondered how long she kept that doggone thing on her nares – it interfered with an otherwise very pretty face.

She led me down the hallway, which opened up to reveal a sunken living room. It was elegantly furnished – a quiet and seemingly luxurious comfort. In the middle, the huge silk – laden sofas formed a rectangle that invitingly faced a fireplace. On top of the mantle was a flat – screen TV showing an Indian music video that the young woman turned off as soon as I sank into a sofa.

"Can I get you something to drink?" she asked.

"Some water please."

She left and I took the chance to look around me some more – nothing unusual except that it felt different, despite the welcoming aroma of some kind of incense or food cooking on a stove somewhere in the background. I had never been to an Indian home before, neither had any of my friends I guess. For a people who had lived in Kenya for such a long time and with whom we shared a history, we had remained strangers and almost always suspicious of each other.

The young woman came back with a glass of cold water, which she placed on the coffee table in front of me. I thanked her and introduced myself and doubtfully asked her if she was Mrs. Mehta.

"No, that's my mother," she laughed. She turned to walk away but then stopped abruptly, looked at me and asked me why I was there. Her eyes, with dark eye shadow and mascara, looked huge, almost too large for her face.

"Your mother called me."

I wanted to say something, some consoling words to one who had just lost a parent, but nothing came to my mind quickly enough.

"Are you a friend of my father?"

"Well, not really. I don't know ..."

"Saranya, that's ok – I'll take it from here," a voice said from behind me.

I turned around to see an older lady, who I now correctly guessed was Mrs. Mehta. She was dressed in a red sari that draped around her all the way to the floor. The girl looked at her mother and then walked off in a huff – a child being shut out from adult conversation and not taking kindly to that.

"Children, these days ... do you have any, Jack?"

I was at a loss but she did not let me answer.

"I'm so sorry to have dragged you here this early. But I did not know what else to do."

"That's quite alright Mrs. Mehta – just tell me what happened ... everything ... anything!"

She sat on a sofa opposite me and clasped her hands on her thighs. Then she took a deep breath and let it out slowly. First, she reached behind her and picked up a photo of her husband and placed it on my lap.

To me he looked like a regular Indian Joe – trimmed beard, thick eyebrows and a grin that exposed a nice set of teeth. His long hair, jet black with strands of gray shining through, cropped and divided in the middle of his head. He was smiling – one of those subtle smiles that are inevitably coerced by an energetic photographer.

I made to hand it back to her but she did not take it.

Instead, she started to relate the story of what had transpired. She told me that she had heard a commotion in the garage but she did not think anything of it at first; her husband usually entertained his friends there, his man – cave she derisively called it. But his paranoid state, a few nights before, and the silence that followed the noise, finally prompted her to check it out. And that's when she found her husband in a pool of blood on the floor of the garage. He had been stabbed severally.

She said that she had tried to stem the bleeding, and then CPR but nothing helped. He died right there in her arms. That's when she had run back to the living room and called the police.

She paused for a minute and then continued.

"I should have asked him more questions ..."

"You can't go blaming yourself now, Mrs. Mehta, you just can't!" I hastened to say.

"I know, but given his state of mind since the week before, I should have."

"What kind of work does – did he do?"

"He was a pharmacist. We have a store in Nairobi."

She handed me a business card. It had his name, a phone number and *Mehta's Drug Emporium* emblazoned across the top in gold writing. On the top right corner, in small print, were the letters MDE. I flipped it over but there was nothing else on the back of it – just a small imprint of a dove – or some kind of bird.

"I still don't know why he asked you to call me," I said. "How did he know me?"

Then I looked at the photo again as if it held a secret I could not see. There was nothing to it. I still could not place him.

"He just said to call you," she started to say but choked up. "Mr. Chidi, please look into it. I don't know what or where to turn from here."

"What time would you say you found him?" I asked, resorting to the usual routine line of questioning.

"It was way past one in the morning. I should say maybe two o'clock…"

"Your daughter, did she see or hear anything?"

"Saranya, she was asleep. But she came running down when she heard me screaming…I tried to shield her from the grisly sight but she insisted…"

She now cried, softy at first and then, it seemed, she allowed herself to bawl. I sat there awkwardly and it was a relief when her daughter came downstairs and rocked her in her arms as they both cried.

"One more question, Mrs. Mehta, if I may. You said he entertained his friends in the garage. Like who are his friends?"

"They were mostly doctors…and his business partners – like William…Mohali; he didn't have many personal friends, really."

She wiped tears from her eyes and her daughter held her tighter. Saranya was about to say something and then stopped.

"Were any of them with him that night?" I asked.

"No, I don't think so…You wouldn't think that they…"

"Mrs. Mehta, I'm not saying anything, just trying to get a clear picture, that's all."

I would have to re – visit this at a later time – she was too distraught for me to ask for more details there and then.

"Mrs. Mehta, I will call you if I have any more questions or if I hear anything that might be of interest. And please accept my condolences."

Though I promised her that I would look into it, I knew that there was not much I could do as an investigative journalist. This was a case for the police, the homicide squad to be exact. It beat me why I had been called in, of all things by the deceased himself!

I let myself out. Once the cool Limuru breeze hit my nostrils, I took a deep breath and then let it out slowly. The crime scene, with the doors cordoned off with yellow tape, was to my right. I walked towards the back and took a peek through a side – window. There was nothing to see here – just a 69 Ford Cortina, a pool table, an old bicycle and some engine parts. I saw what appeared to be oil stains and a pool of drying blood on the floor. I walked the perimeter of the garage – there were no signs of a forced entry.

Down the driveway, I looked back at the house and saw Mrs. Mehta and her daughter looking at me through one of the windows. I waved at them, turned around and walked off, oddly feeling like a trespasser. I felt bad for them, pinning their hopes on me, knowing that I was not going to be of much help.

Once I passed the country club, I decided to stop at the Tigoni Police station – perhaps whoever had been assigned to the case had something to say.

After a brisk walk, I was standing in front of the station – an old, dirty and ominous – looking building. Despite its small size and signs of heavy and constant volume, I was struck by how quiet and unassuming it was. Well, ignoring the instituted tents that housed arrestees before they were transported to the various magistrates' courts for trial or sentencing, it almost looked abandoned.

To the side of the building was a small field where in days past I had seen officers playing soccer between shifts. Now, it was a graveyard for their retired dilapidated Land Rovers and Cruisers.

I walked up the steps, opened a wooden door and entered the reception area. It was a rather large room with no furniture, save for a small bookshelf propped against a corner wall with old pamphlets of missing persons and two long wooden benches, one in front of the other like church pews.

To the far corner of the room, an old blue phone booth, complete with a tattered phonebook hanging on a metallic chain, stood oddly by, a relic of times past. The ambiance was cold and very uninviting but then again, this is not a place you came calling on social visits.

A toilet flushed and I turned around quickly – unexpected noises alarm me. A tall, seemingly athletic officer appeared from a side door. I did not know him. I was about to extend my hand in greeting out of habit but quickly changed my mind when I saw him busy adjusting his trousers and fiddling with his belt. He walked right up and stood in front of me, sizing me up and then sucked on his teeth. On the wall behind him, just above a long filing cabinet over – laden with papers and files, was the portrait copy of President Joakim, with that surreptitious smile on his lips.

"What kind of complaint are you making today?" he asked, with a tone meant to let me know that he was in charge.

"My name is Jack. Jack Chidi. I am an investigative journalist with the *Daily Grind*."

He took a good look at me and then his face softened into an amiable smile.

"Ah yes, the journalist, I have read your work."

He extended his hand right into mine. His smile told me that he was a fan – I have quite a following. Screw hygiene! His grip was firm, almost rough, perhaps driven by excitement.

"Jeremy Nyongesa is the name," he introduced himself with a toothy smile. "But call me Jerry like the American comedian – Seinfeld, eh?"

I hesitated, not sure how to react to the American thing.

"What can I do for you?" he continued.

"I am here about a reported incident regarding a Vishal Mehta."

"Mehta!" he exclaimed, giving me the lookover. "You have to be more specific. Do you want to record a statement about Mehta's death?"

"No, I want to talk to someone familiar with the case ... to ask a few questions, you know, the usual."

"I don't think it has been assigned to anyone as yet."

"Well, is there anything you can tell me ... you know, murder weapon, suspects ... anything you can tell me, Jerry?"

"I really can't tell you much," he said and looked behind him as if to make sure that there was no one listening before he continued. "They found a knife, right next to him."

I pulled out my note pad and placed it on the counter. As I fumbled for a pen, Jerry pushed my pad slowly back towards me – as if to say it was all off the record. I nodded to show him I understood.

"Did they find any prints on it?" I asked.

Jerry shot a cursory glance behind him again. Just when he was about to say something, a fully uniformed officer came bustling through the door. He had a small afro hairstyle with little tufts of gray creeping in. He could not have been older that fifty but his rounded cheeks gave him a youthful exuberance that did not match the gray hair. He walked up and stood in front of me, nose to nose. To him, I guess, I had come to pile up more police work on an already understaffed department. To me, he was just a bore with bad breath.

"Sir, this is Jack Chidi with the *Daily Grind,*" Jerry hastened to explain. "He is here about the Vishal case."

"Is he?"

"Jack, this is my boss, OCPD Bernard Lelo."

He looked at me one more time, bad breadth and all, and then walked behind the counter.

"It used to be the lawyers, now it's the media," Lelo said with a sneer. "How do you even know about this? The body is hardly cold."

I did not care for his insinuation but I was not about to tell him that Mrs. Mehta had called me. If I had learned anything from working with Bulldog, it was that you never ever volunteer information to a police officer.

"How exactly did you sniff out this murder?" He placed his middle finger on his nose for emphasis. He was using the oldest trick in the book to give me the finger.

"We have our sources" I shot out defensively.

Damn! We had started out on the wrong foot and there was no remedying the situation. I don't know what it was with cops: they either took to me the first time they laid eyes on me or they hated me. There was no in – between.

"Sources, huh? Well, so do the police, Mr. Chidi. But at this moment we are not talking to the media unless they have something to help us with our investigations."

"But you did say it's a murder?"

"I don't know anyone that can stab themselves to death, but perhaps you do, being a journalist and all."

"There's no need for that, Sir. I am just trying to get some infor…"

"Listen here, we are on top of this. Just go home and let us do our job."

He looked very self – assured, an almost unshakeable faith in his oath to uphold the law. He reminded me of those over – zealous police officers who planted evidence on suspects just so they could make an arrest. His red eyes danced on my face again but I held his gaze. Then he smiled, ever so slightly.

"So, unless you have something to help us, we ask that you leave," he said, waving his short, stubby fingers at me.

He walked back to his office.

Jerry stood there briefly but I knew that he was not going to be divulging any more information – not with Stubby within ear shot and breathing down his neck. I quickly reached into my pocket and pulled out my business card. On the back I scribbled, 'Limuru Ndeiya, Five O'clock' and slid it out to him. He looked at it, palmed it carefully and thrust it in his pocket before turning back to see if Stubby was back.

I left and walked towards the bus stop, briefly stopping at the Tigoni Stores to buy some gum. Then I caught a matatu back to Limuru from where I boarded a bus to town.

Chapter Two

I found Bulldog in his office. Nothing strange about that! One was always sure to find Bulldog waiting if there was a new story to be sniffed out.

"Aye, Jack Chidi reporting for duty, Sir!"

He did not respond to my salutation but instead wagged his index finger playfully then beckoned me to take a seat. His office was laden with newspapers and magazines and I was not sure whether he wanted me to move them aside or sit on the pile. Not to disorganize his clutter, I sat on it, balancing myself delicately between paper and more paper.

"Why don't you just move that crap out of the way?" he growled.

I didn't answer him. It was a waste of time – this is how he was. He looked around and then, after taking stock, he asked, grumpily:

"So, what did you find?"

I told him about the phone call again, Mrs. Mehta, her daughter Saranya and my visit to the police station, with Stubby and Jerry. He listened, all the while nodding his head and mumbling some affirmations.

"Not much, but there is a story there," he said patronizingly.

Congratulations, genius, I thought to myself. There were times when I felt like cursing him out.

"I still don't know why she called me, or even when or why her husband asked her to call," I said trying to go it another way.

"Maybe they wanted the story to come out."

"What story?"

"That's where you come in," he said.

Then he leaned forward and clicked on his computer, signaling that he was done with me.

I walked into my office, logged onto my computer and began a search for Vishal Mehta. He was listed as the proprietor of Mehta's Drug Emporium. He had been in business for a while, operating from the same location on Muindi Mbingu Street before moving his operations to Parklands. There was not much else to go by.

If Mehta had come home afraid for his life, then he knew that whoever was threatening him intended to carry it through. But why had he not gone to the authorities? But perhaps Mrs. Mehta had made it all up. If so, why? What did she have to gain by dragging me into this? Whatever the case, I was not going to rule anything out just yet.

What would have been a routine morning for me had come with intrigues.

I called Mrs. Mehta's house number after lunch. I figured that ample time had passed and she had collected herself a little bit. It rang for a while before someone picked it up.

"Could I please speak with Mrs. Mehta?"

"She is not in at the moment," a woman answered. "May I know who is calling?"

"Yes, my name is Jack Chidi," I said unsure if it was Saranya or not.

"Oh, I remember you," she replied. "You're the journalist who came by this morning."

"Saranya, how are you holding up?" I said, trying to sound cheerful so as to make up for my earlier lack of empathetic words.

"I'm fine," she answered. "I guess I'm doing as well as could be expected under the circumstances."

"I know these are hard times, Saranya, and if there is anything I can do, please let me know."

I heard her take a deep breath and waited to hear her response.

"Thanks," she said briefly.

"When do you expect that your mother will be back?"

"I don't know."

"You just hung in there."

"Ok," she said and before I could leave any message for her mother, she hung up.

I had wanted to tell her that it would be all right, but that would have been a lie. I had lost my father many years ago. I was very young at the time and did not know him well. Yet, these many years later, it still felt unreal at times. All the same, I felt a sense of solidarity with her – the loss of a father is not an easy thing to overcome. I was about to call again to say so when Otieno, my colleague and drinking buddy, came bustling in.

"Hey Chidi, where you been all day, man?"

He wore his trademark broad smile on the face. I often wondered how anyone could always look this cheerful – but he always brightened up my day.

"Man, I went up to Tigoni to see this Indian woman who called me early this morning."

He looked at me like I had just stolen a piece of candy.

"Quit playing, man! An Indian woman called you?"

"Yeah man, she called me for help."

"First of all, you don't know any Indians and secondly, since when did Indians call anyone but their own for help?"

"I know. But she called me."

"Sure she did!"

"It was about her dead husband."

"Or her resurrected father, what next?"

"So you think I'm lying."

"No, tell me all about it."

So I told Otieno about Mrs. Mehta's call and what she had said about her husband's frantic state of mind days before he died and about Saranya who was young and ... but he cut me short.

"Get outta here!" he said, faking an American accent, his eyes brimming with excitement. "So you say that he knew he was going to get it?"

"Sounds like it."

He then looked at me from the corner of his eyes and asked, mockingly, "Did she kill him you think?"

"No, well, I don't think so but get this: her husband was the one who asked her to call me should something happen to him!"

"Is that so?"

"So she said."

"She could be lying, you know."

"Then why would she call me?"

Otieno was quiet for a second and then asked, "Is she good looking?"

"The mother or the daughter?" I asked, puzzled. "What are you getting at?"

"Well is she or is she not?"

I ignored him but I told him that I was heading out to Limuru to meet Jerry after work.

"Jerry?" he replied. "Now who's that?"

"A cop with the Tigoni police department..."

"Oh, in that case I'm going with you."

"Be my guest."

*****

Limuru Ndeiya was quite busy for a weekday and the waiter was having a hard time taking orders but before too long we were caressing cold tuskers. There is something to say about a cold one, I was saying to Otieno, but I did not finish. He wasn't smiling. This was the first time we had been back here since the night of Dr. Kizito's murder. The good doctor was one of the victims in a case Otieno and I had worked on together and one that had taken us to the very depths of evil. But that, as I've said, is another story that he and I preferred to bury in the past.

A most heart–wrenching part of the story was the doctor's sister, Irene, who had come to visit with him. Instead of vacationing in Mombasa like they had planned, she ended up burying her brother. After his burial, she had returned to Texas – to a husband and two kids. I had kept in touch with her with the occasional email and not much else.

I did not know what to say to Otieno. This was a subject that we had avoided but one that was still raw and fresh like the morning dew.

I ordered a kilo of roast goat with a side dish of potatoes and *kachumbari*. This mixture of chili, green peppers, tomatoes and cilantro always went well with roast goat. I knew this would cheer Otieno right up and it did!

"So, I am finally meeting her next Saturday," I started, and suddenly he was all ears.

"The Indian woman?"

"No!"

It was Meredith. Although we spoke regularly on the phone, somehow, she and I had kept away from each other, though not by design. She worked as a waitress at the New London Grill in Nairobi and had just finished her Hotel Management training at Utalii College on the way to Kenyatta University. I liked her – and it was clear she was into me but we had not made that move just yet, well until now.

"Man, you are quite something if I may say so. In fact you should have moved to the desert already – you just can't starve yourself through life the way you do," he said, laughing heartily, and all the while tapping on the counter for emphasis. "It's not natural."

"Man, I need to talk to Akinyi about your teasing me like this!" I protested.

"Why are you always bringing my wife into these discussions?"

Otieno and Akinyi had been married for some time now and they got along just fine – well, as long as he behaved himself. With three children between them – two from Akinyi's previous marriage and one together – they made it work but it was not easy. Otieno enjoyed his drink a little bit too much and Akinyi was suspicious that it was not the only thing he was enjoying away from home.

I challenged Otieno to a pool game but just when he was about to rack the balls on the table, Jerry walked in.

"Hello, Mr. Chidi!"

"Just call me Jack," I answered, turning to welcome him. "This here is my friend Otieno. Otieno, this is Jeremy…"

"Jerry, please – like Jerry Seinfeld," he insisted and we all laughed.

Jerry then sat down beside me and looked around the bar. He was just a regular thirty – something – guy without his police uniform. But his wide face showed signs of tough living and I wondered how he ended up at the police academy. He was not as lean as he had looked at the station but rather athletic without trying – the kind that my boxing coach used to call a natural.

"How is it going?" I asked him.

He looked back at me and then at Otieno and smiled. The waiter came over and Jerry ordered a soda.

"Nothing against alcohol," he apologized. "It's only my strong Christian upbringing."

He must have seen my facial expression and the laughter I could barely hold in.

"It's no laughing matter," he commented.

"Praise the Lord!" Otieno chimed in, lifting up his glass to toast.

We all three laughed and as the laughter subsided, I got down to business.

"Jerry, what's going on with the Mehta case?"

He did not answer immediately and Otieno jumped in by way of encouragement.

"Just so you know whatever you tell us is in confidence."

That had always been my number one rule – establish working parameters with your sources.

"Thank you for the reassurance," Jerry smiled. "I don't want any of this coming back to me. My boss does not like anything going out of the station."

I knew what he was talking about – there were to be no leaks in an ongoing investigation.

"So what do you guys think happened?" I asked rather anxiously.

For no apparent reason, I wanted this whole thing to wrap up quickly and I hoped the police would get to the bottom of it; the Mehta's needed some kind of closure.

"Well, Mehtas wife called around Two – thirty in the morning. I myself took the report. She said she had heard commotion in the garage at about midnight but thought nothing of it since her husband usually hangs out there with his friends. She then said that when she woke up at around One and realized that her husband had not come to bed, she walked over to the garage to see what was going on and that's when she found him."

"She waited a whole hour to call?" Otieno asked, and I knew what he was already thinking.

"What else?"

Jerry, assuming a conspiratorial look, whispered that Mehta had been stabbed to death and his wife had told them she had picked up the murder weapon – actually pulled it out of him.

He looked around again as if to make sure that he could not be overheard.

"There is another piece of evidence: a small clover – shaped diamond stud, like an earring, you know. He was holding it in his right hand – all covered in his blood. We know it must be hers."

"Whose?" I asked.

"Mrs. Mehta, of course!" he answered. "She said it herself. It was must have fallen off when she was trying to resuscitate him."

His version of what had happened corroborated Mrs. Mehta's story. And it did not look good for her – she had this murder written all over her. The knife with her fingerprints, the earring …All this didn't look good. The only question was: why would she kill him?

"Have they lifted any fingerprints on the murder weapon and do you have any other suspects?" I asked, my heart suddenly going into overdrive.

"The knife is being processed for prints but as far as I know, at this stage his wife is the primary suspect – standard protocol. We always suspect everyone and then we use the process of elimination until we are left with those with both opportunity and motive."

"And the girl?" I asked, alarmed for no reason.

"Her alibi checked out," Jerry replied. "She was asleep when this whole thing went down – besides, the girl gains nothing from her father's death. Everything points to the mother – the knife, the blood on her clothes, opportunity… It's not looking good for her."

"Anything else, Jerry?"

"Not really," he answered. Then he seemed to have an afterthought before proceeding. "But there were some foot prints, a size four. We think maybe some kid from the nearby school climbed over the perimeter fence earlier on to perhaps retrieve a ball by the garage or something of the sort. You know what kids are like."

There was nothing else Jerry could give us. I thanked him for his time. Before he left, he asked me if what he had told us was going to be in the papers.

"Not yet," I reassured him. "But why?"

"Oh, nothing!" he shook his head and smiled. "I just wanted to make sure I get a copy, without any mention of my name, of course!"

Chapter Three

Mrs. Mehta's arrest was all over the newspapers the following morning. In a statement issued by the Tigoni Police and confirmed by a Senior Detective from the CID Headquarters in Nairobi, her fingerprints matched those on the murder weapon. Bloodstains on one of her saris matched that of the victim.

She would appear in front of the Kiambu Municipal Magistrate later that afternoon for arraignment. Her charges: first-degree murder, aggravated assault with a deadly weapon, and conspiracy to cover up a crime.

"It seems like the State has all it needs for a conviction," Otieno said.

"Well, anything is possible," I answered without conviction. I kind of expected that she would be arrested but from how she had presented herself to me, I was not at all convinced that she did it. I knew investigators sometimes rushed to judgment, or overlooked critical pieces of evidence in an overzealous quest for a conviction, but our legal system was slowly changing for the better.

"Who's that guy in America who had his dick cut off by his wife?" Otieno said, suddenly.

I remembered the story well.

"Yeah, some guy named Bobbitt or some funny name like that."

"Do you know that for several months after that I watched Akinyi like a hawk? I even started sleeping on my belly," Otieno said, feigning seriousness.

"But what's Bobbitt got to do with anything?" I asked after some laughter.

"Well, I bring that up to say that Mrs. Mehta could have snapped and acted out of frustration or anger."

"Point well taken but I'm not calling it in just yet."

I asked him if he wanted to accompany me to Mrs. Mehta's arraignment.

"It shouldn't take long and afterwards we can pass by The Nova for some *choma* and a cold one."

He couldn't say resist that. So he left to get his corduroy jacket while I checked my email. I was still chuckling at his story when he came back and we left the building. After a brisk walk through the lunchtime crowd, we were sitting in a *matatu* headed for Kiambu.

The rolling hills of tea estates and coffee plantations that carpet the outskirts of Kiambu belie that it is a burgeoning cosmopolitan town with a reputation for violence – from marauding gangs of young men and women trying to find their place in the world, to a ruthless business class of shady traders and political conmen who preyed on passersby and residents alike.

It was also home to some very ingenious pioneers – like my friend, Solomon, who had convinced the Municipal Council to allow his consulting company, Nature's House, to install wind turbines on government lands and solar panels in all government buildings under the jurisdiction of the Municipality.

I first met Solomon to cover a story on Nature's House. We had talked for hours after the interview and later, he had invited me to a pre – wedding party he was throwing for an employee's daughter. First, he had taken me around his property – a three – acre farm that he was transforming into an organic oasis of sustainable living.

I had since visited with Solomon several times at his Kiambu office and we had become fast friends – a man I could count on in times of need. He also knew people in high places, which came in handy on occasions when I needed an introduction to someone or just some personal information.

On our way to the courthouse, I called him and he agreed to meet us as soon as we were done.

"And tell Otieno that I have no stories for him," he added, laughing.

He always teased Otieno about his interest in other people's sex – life but it was indeed Solomon who could not wait to churn out a tale or two of his latest exploits – real or imagined.

The Kiambu courthouse, the center for all kinds of licensing, taxes, civil and criminal cases, teemed with people from all walks of life who waited patiently for their allotted cases to come up for mention. Outside, the bustle and hustle of life raged on while police cars, with sirens blaring, brought in more accused and prisons cars shortly after escorted the condemned to prison.

The criminal court was a small room with wooden benches for the public; a rather innocuous table for the lawyers; a dock for witnesses and, in the front, the judge's bench behind which, on the wall, hung a portrait of President Joachim, presiding over the proceedings. That was all standard for most courts, but what got to me at Kiambu was a stench – a putrid smell of dust, urine and utter despair.

We sat down on one of the backbenches and soon every available seat was taken. Most of the people here had no bearing on the case whatsoever: some came for entertainment; others to while away their lunch hours; and only a few were family and friends. I looked around. The prosecutor, a tall man with a neatly shaven beard was talking excitedly to one of his colleagues about a forthcoming golf tournament.

Saranya sat quietly between two Asian women, one of whom wore a business suit. They were hunched over, going through some paper work quietly, except the occasional whisper amongst themselves. Directly behind them was a really tall and gawky black man. Perhaps his imposing size would not have stood out had it not been for the shortest Asian man I had ever laid my eyes on – a Man – child, I said to myself.

There was a collective murmur in the courtroom when one of the doors opened and Mrs. Mehta was brought in with her hands and feet tethered like a cow being led to slaughter. She struggled to walk between two armed guards who marched on stoically – just another day at the office. She looked so frail and weak, hardly the picture of a murderer and husband – killer.

From the loud murmurs in court, I guessed I was not alone in wondering whether all the show of force was necessary for such a small woman who seemed in no way a danger to society. I wondered if people would have reacted the same way had she been my mother – a black woman accused of killing her husband for no known reason.

As soon as she sat down, Saranya walked over and gave her a hug before the guards pulled her away and marched her mother to her seat. The magistrate walked in. Everyone in the courtroom stood up as directed by the bailiff. After the Magistrate settled in her seat, she asked us to be seated. Long after we had settled down, the dust we had all stirred up danced in the sun's rays like irritating flies.

After sounding the gavel and asking for quiet, Justice Ida read the charges against Mrs. Mehta and asked for her plea. The Indian woman in a business suit stood up and introduced herself as the family lawyer representing Mrs. Mehta and entered a plea of "Not Guilty."

Then she immediately moved to have Mrs. Mehta released on her own recognizance but the prosecutor objected, arguing that the accused was a flight risk. This was not clear to the magistrate who asked, with a smile, whether he meant because of her Asian heritage or because of the evidence pointing to her guilt.

"Well, I would hate to have to look for her if she fled to India – I would not even recognize her, but my objection is more prejudiced by the irrefutable evidence we have that will prove her guilt."

"I object!" protested the defense lawyer. "That is a reckless statement to make. Mrs. Mehta is a Kenyan citizen. So why would she flee to India? Secondly, your honor, she is presumed innocent under the law."

"Your honor, all I am saying is that given her connections, her wealth and the nature of the crime of which she is being charged and the overwhelming evidence against her, she would be a fool not to make a break for it," insisted the prosecutor.

He said they had her fingerprints on the murder weapon, she had the opportunity and motive and lastly, he said with an indulgent smile, "She has more resources and more reasons to flee faster than OJ Simpson."

Some in the crowd fell out in laughter, which prompted the Magistrate to give a stern lecture on court decorum, followed by a threat.

"I will not hesitate to clear my courtroom. There will be no further such outbursts."

Defense then gave a moving testament to her client's credentials as a community organizer, to her selfless work on HIV prevention, her philanthropic work with orphans and the mentally challenged.

"She is a true champion of women's rights, Your Honor, and in spite of all the things she has done for the Kenyan community, she has never claimed glory or notoriety. She is a loving mother, a loving wife and a true patriot. What we have here is a rush to judgment and it should not be allowed to stand. The police have not conducted a thorough investigation but instead they have rushed to throw the book and condemn a poor Indian woman."

"I thought you said she was a Kenyan National," the prosecutor quipped, to more laughter, which quickly faded out following an admonishing look from the Magistrate.

The defense attorney ignored him and continued to lambast the police for what she called shoddy work but the Magistrate was unmoved by her eloquence. She remanded Mrs. Mehta back into police custody and ordered her to stand trial for the murder of her husband on a date to be decided.

After Justice Ida left her bench, Mrs. Mehta was whisked away but not before she looked around the court, at her daughter, her legal counsel and, just as she was about to exit the door, our eyes met. I tried to smile at her, to let her know that I was fulfilling my promise, but her eyes had lost that luster of hope.

I left Otieno seated and walked over to the defense table to meet the team. Man – child and his partner had moved over to the side of the courthouse on their way out. I extended my hand to Saranya who looked up at me, her eyes filled with sadness. I thought she was going to breakdown and cry but she composed herself and introduced me to the lead counsel, Dipti Shah and her assistant, Anita Gore.

"May I have a word with you in private?" I asked Dipti.

"Sure. Is there a place we can talk?"

I told her I was headed to the Red Nova and if she did not mind she could meet me there.

"Give me about half an hour," she consented without hesitation.

As I was leaving, I caught sight of the peculiar couple again: the tall man was hunched over, listening to Man – child. Something about this odd couple made me uneasy for no reason whatsoever. I nudged Otieno but he was also staring at them. The anomalous couple looked our way, maybe sensing our curiosity. We made it to the door and walked out just in time to avoid an awkward situation.

The Nova was almost empty when Otieno and I got there. Joe, the manager – owner came to greet us. He showed us to a table at the far end of the bar. Right behind us was a small stage on which the house – band played on weekends and some evenings. We ordered chips and sausage and a soda to wash it down. The order came and we devoured our lunch like some hungry wolves and shortly after, Dipti and her assistant walked in.

I don't know what it was but there was something about her that looked odd – perhaps it was the business suit since I had never seen an Indian woman in anything but a sari. She had long eyebrows, well – polished make – up and she smelled good. I wondered if she had a husband or boyfriend – it was just my mind wandering.

"I hope you saved some chips for me," she said. Her voice was soft and cajoling, a different tone altogether, not at all like the one at the courtroom.

"Otieno here decided to polish everything," I said by way of introduction. "Don't let his scrawny frame fool you."

Otieno protested, all the while flashing that big grin of his.

"Dipti, please don't listen to Jack," he said. "I hardly touched a thing!" he added as he smacked his telltale oily lips.

Dipti looked at him and burst out laughing. She had a nice set of teeth on her, which accentuated her prominent cheekbones. Her eyes – alive and sharp, were inviting – not in a sexual way yet inviting nonetheless.

"It's okay," she said. "We will have some tea and get lunch back at the office. Shall we get down to business?"

"Yes, please, I wanted to talk to you about this…" I started but she cut me short.

"Mrs. Mehta told me about the phone call. But you did not know Vishal Mehta, did you?"

"No, I didn't, but that's the thing," I admitted. "Why do you think he wanted me on the case?"

"Perhaps we can start from the beginning?" she suggested.

I guessed she was one of those people who like order, so I obliged her. Her assistant pulled out a folder and handed it to her. She looked it over and then at me before her eyes rested on Otieno.

"Whatever we say here stays with us – I'm sure you understand," but before we could answer, she continued.

"What we have here is a miscarriage of justice. The police have the wrong person."

"Of course!" Otieno said, quite meaninglessly.

I knew what he was thinking but I let her continue. She told us there was something sinister in the manner in which the police had handled the case, the way they contaminated evidence and refused to investigate, instead taking the easy way out of a murder investigation. What did Mrs. Mehta have to gain by killing her husband at home in their own garage? People who could afford it usually hired hit men to carry out such a deed – and in Kenya, they were a dime a dozen – very cost effective, don't you agree?"

Otieno was about to say something but I nudged him in the ribs, suggesting we needed to hear her out.

"There was a small life insurance policy, hardly enough to cover cremation costs and other expenses. They are already wealthy so she is clearly not interested in such a small amount. Secondly, she does not know anything about running a pharmacy nor does she gain by inheriting their material possessions – the house and another rental property in Kileleshwa – because she is in fact the registered owner. This is clearly a case of a hurried and botched investigation – in fact I dare call it a frame. The said motive is highly improbable and the opportunity is questionable."

"So what do you think happened since all you have is conjecture?" I asked and almost regretted my tone – it was accusing and I guessed deep down I had started believing that Mrs. Mehta had actually killed her husband for the same reasons Dipti was putting across to prove her innocence.

"Do you think that small woman you saw in there could have overpowered such a strong man?" she asked and then looked at Otieno before shifting her eyes to me.

"Well, how does she account for the time it took her to call the police after she found...?"

"Come on now, Jack!" she countered immediately. "She tried to save her husband, trying to stop the bleeding and finally, when she realized he was gone, she called the police. Now the question should be how long the police took to get from the station to her house – it's not a long walk, and why they did not scour the area to look for suspects."

"Which still leaves us with the question of motive and opportunity," Otieno now chimed in.

"That is where we are," Dipti admitted. "But I'm telling you, Mrs. Mehta did not do this. The real killer is still out there!" she added emphatically.

I wanted to believe her but one cannot argue against evidence. My skepticism was understandable – and I would not let it deter me from digging a little deeper. I owed Mrs. Mehta, her daughter Saranya, and the dead husband that much.

"Can you think of anyone who would want him dead?" I asked after a pause in our conversation.

"Not really, but one can make enemies quickly in this country. This murder, anyway you cut it, was driven by some twisted sense of justice or greed. The same two forces could drive a premeditated murder or a spontaneous killing, you know. The only problem is that no one knows what Mehta had gotten himself into – at least not yet."

"Was he into politics at all?" Otieno asked, seemingly taking the bait.

Dipti shook her head from side to side.

"Oh, no, no political enemies, he hated politics," she replied. "All he ever wanted was to make enough money for his retirement. But, gentlemen, whatever we need to do we need to do it fast!"

I thought of Mrs. Mehta, sitting by herself in a cold cell – her life hanging on what we did or did not do. The prosecutor had the murder weapon, Mrs. Mehta had the opportunity – they just needed to prove the motive and she was toast.

Although Dipti sounded thorough and her thoughts were well laid out, she did not allude to what I had already concluded: that Mehta wanted me to expose some deep shit should his life come to an abrupt end. Yet, still, what if Mrs. Mehta was playing victim to a crime she had orchestrated? But was she really capable of such intrigue?

What was clear from the way Dipti drew me into her reasoning was that she hoped I might write a piece from her angle, appeal to the public. Not a bad place to start but I needed more meat for that kind of story than we already had – Bulldog would not let it run with just this conjecture.

"Why do you think she, well, that her husband asked her to call me?" I asked.

"I'm not sure but you have quite a following, you know. You do some good work, Jack, especially your last case – the one with, what's his name ... and that woman…the coroner. You know how these things work – police negligence and corruption run deep in this country."

She was referring to the case that became known as City Murders. It was a case that had brought me no small share of notoriety.

"I didn't know I had made such an impression on…"

"A modest celebrity!" Dipti said as she pulled her briefcase shut.

Then as she and her assistant stood up to leave, she offered to share any new information with me as soon as she got it and I also promised to stay in touch.

"About Saranya – is there a place or friend she can stay with in the meantime?" I asked, concerned for her sanity in being left at their house by herself.

"Oh, she is staying with me for now," Dipti reassured me. "But thanks Jack, thanks for asking."

Hardly had they stepped out of the door when Solomon came sauntering in with his boisterous presence and immediately ordered a welcome round of drinks.

Chapter Four

Since I was not doing much in the office, I decided to go over to the Mehta's Drug Emporium Pharmacy. I pulled out his business card and looked at the address – it was located on 3rd Avenue, Parklands, not very far from my office. I grabbed my jacket and headed out. A few minutes later, I was on a bus to Parklands, listening to an old Kalamashaka tune.

My stop came quickly and I alighted from the bus and started down 3rd Avenue. Parklands was once the designated residential area for colonial civil servants. I still don't know how it had changed and become disproportionately Indian.

Mehta's Drug Emporium was located on the first floor of a three – storied brick building almost at the end of the street. It stood out because of its strange mixture of colors with no discernible pattern as far as I could tell. I crossed the front parking lot, walked to the huge glass doors and let myself in. The walls were covered with colorful and vibrant posters carrying advertisements for pharmaceuticals, health warnings from the Kenya Medical Research Institute and slogans of the ages – old anti – smoking campaign.

There was no one behind the counter but there was a small bell with instructions to ring it for assistance. I tapped it twice with my index finger, took a step back and looked around. There was a waiting area – brown leather couches and a coffee table, a small bookshelf stacked with medical journals and old copies of *Newsweek, Times Magazine* and *Golf Now.*

I sat down and pulled out the golf magazine. My eyes rested on a photo essay on Tiger Woods, sequencing his full swing and giving some tips on how to play from sand bunkers. I was soon absorbed, trying to imagine these shots.

"Welcome to MDE, sir," a voice said, startling me from my absorption in the golfing world. "What can we do for you today?"

I looked up. I was still a little taken back. I had not expected to see a white woman in Parklands – an Indian, yes, or even a black woman but never a white woman. Parklands was a far cry from Karen – the whitest part of Nairobi. I had come to associate certain neighborhoods with certain types. Parklands was Indian country for all practical purposes and they remained almost separated from other nationalities – whether by design or circumstance, it was hard to say, especially these many years after independence. I was now thinking that it was their treatment of African workers that at times left something to be desired.

But it was not just the Indians who were the culprits here. Otieno had done an investigative report comparing how Asian and African merchants treated their African employees. The choice of pejoratives may have been different but the contempt was there all the same. But there was a difference in how the workers reacted. With their abusive African employers, the workers did not return insult for insult. But to the Asian, they responded with as much venom and pejoratives. Which made me think of another angle to my murder mystery: could a disgruntled employee have decided they had had enough of insults from the Mehtas and decided to respond with more than words?

I had to pull myself back from this mental digression to where I was. The white woman was smiling, showing a nice set of pearls. Her hair was short and neatly cropped. She was not wearing the white lab – coat I had come to associate with pharmacies and hospitals. Instead, she was smartly dressed – a tight black skirt, black high heels with stockings that made her legs look longer and a cream blouse buttoned up all the way to the neck. I stood up and extended my hand to her. She had soft hands – almost too soft.

"My name is Jack Chidi," I introduced myself formally. "I had called – I want to speak with the manager."

"Oh, I see. What is this about, if I may ask?"

"Are you the manager – Ms …?"

"Jones…Olivia Jones," she answered.

She was still smiling but I could see the corners of the smile dissipate and then she firmly told me that she was indeed the manager as if to dispel any doubts I might have had.

"Please follow me to my office," she said and turned around towards a side door that opened up to a corridor. Three doors down, we walked into a magnificent office where she sat down behind an enormous mahogany desk.

"Can I get you anything to drink, Mr. Chidi?" she offered, her smile having returned.

I asked for some water. She pressed on the intercom and ordered for a coffee and water. Then she crossed her arms on her chest and breathed out in readiness for what I was about say.

"So, what can I do for you?" she asked guardedly.

"It's about Vishal Mehta," I went straight to the point. "I am from the Press – the *Daily Grind* to be precise."

Then I pulled out a pen and my notebook and started scribbling – I doodle a lot when I'm not sure about something but it helps me focus.

"Ah, yes," she answered casually. "It came as a shock to us. We are still at a loss and we are not even sure how to react to this tragedy."

Her face lost that smile and she sounded sincere. I stared at her and waited for what else she was going to say.

"What does his passing have to do with you and your paper?" she asked.

She was looking right at me – her eyes sad but inquisitive.

"I am trying to piece together the events leading up to his death… there is something there…"

"Something like what?" she asked, almost too abruptly and then caught herself, adding: "Please continue."

"I was just saying that there is something amiss," I said vaguely, fishing for any slip that might tell me something I could clutch on.

"What do you mean?" she flung her arms around, for no apparent reason.

She reminded me of those clerks in government offices who only show up to work just for a paycheck.

"These past few days, did he seem agitated, you know, out of sorts or what have you?"

"Not that I noticed – but he was always quiet – said hello and all that but he kept to himself – a really nice fellow. What a shame!"

I looked around her office again. There were numerous items of the usual pharmaceutical literature, pens, and note pads on her desk. On one side of the wall was one of those magnetic calendars with some dates circled as reminders.

Directly behind her was a huge map of the world – with pins stuck on it – Saudi Arabia, United States, Canada and several European countries – places she had visited or perhaps wanted to visit in the future, I thought to myself. I had not done much travel myself and I envied her that much.

"What exactly was the nature of his work?" I asked, taking in as much of her office as I could.

Her desk was neatly laid out, with a laptop in front of her and two desktop computers on each side. All these sat on a glass pane under which I spotted travel brochures – the ones you get at a travel agency.

"Really?" she expressed surprise. "You come to a pharmacy and you ask what we do here?"

"No, I meant what was his day – to – day work here? Was it research or manufacturing and packaging?"

"Mr. Chidi, I really cannot tell you that," she answered as if alarmed. "This is a pharmacy and we have deals with all kinds of pharmaceutical companies from all over the world."

She moved her arms and directed me to the world map, and then continued: "He made those deals in his office so I cannot tell you what he did all day now, can I?" she asked with a sharpness that bordered on sarcasm.

She needed to drop the attitude but I decided to press on.

"What about his business partners, let's see…" I looked at my note pad… "Ah, yes, William and …?"

"Oh, no! I cannot discuss company details with you. Besides, the police have already charged Mrs. Mehta with the murder of her husband, haven't they?"

"And what do you think about that?" Do you think she was the kind of woman who would…?"

"I am not in law – enforcement but I am sure the police must have had good reason before they arrested her."

With that, she abruptly stood up to show me the way out. As I followed her down the corridor, I asked if I could look into Mehta's office but I knew the answer even before I finished asking the question.

"Good day, Mr. Chidi," she said icily.

I walked out and headed to the bus stop. She had not given me much at all. I needed something else – a different lead. I just had to keep digging.

It was time to curry a favor. I called Detective Felix Dube and we agreed to meet later on.

*****

I met Dube at The Corner House Den after work. It was his favorite joint and I soon understood why. The waitresses in skimpy outfits that revealed more than they covered were all over him, attentive and unabashedly flirtatious.

"Hey, Chidi, long time, I was wondering when you would call."

He sounded enthusiastic but his facial expression did not match his voice. I had found it useful not to take anything for granted when dealing with the law. They gave as much as they needed to give and although it was frustrating at times, I was careful not to act with any sense of entitlement.

I pulled up a chair and sat across the table from him. A waitress came and I ordered a cup of tea.

"What!" Dube protested. "Man, you drinking tea! Uh uh…get the man a cold one. It's on me."

"Okay, Tusker, then," I conceded.

He did not have to twist my arm.

"Oh, and get me another Walker, on the rocks if you please!"

He then leaned back on his chair and gave me a once over – as if he was trying to read me. But I chose to wait for him to break the ice and say something, anything at all. He was now ogling at a girl sitting at a table to our left. He tried to catch her attention but she ignored him. He wiped his lips with the back of his hand and turned back to me.

"I never really got to thank you properly after our last case," he started.

He was referring to the City Murders but I did not want to go there. It was a case I had tried hard to put behind me but it was always showing up when I least wanted it.

"I need you to do something for me, a favor," I started, not knowing exactly how to broach the subject – but he owed me big time and I was glad he remembered.

He leaned forward looking all – serious and beckoned me to get closer, like he was going to let me in on a big secret.

"You want me to shoot someone for you?" he asked, then broke into genuine laughter. "You should see your face!"

He continued laughing for a minute before he realized that I had not joined him. After all I did not know him that well. To me he was just a work in progress, not a bosom buddy like Otieno.

"Sorry, Jack. It's a joke…"

An awkward silence ensued and I was glad when the waitress returned with our drinks.

By then the place was packed almost to capacity. The loud din, the music, the laughter and the potpourri of perfumes, food and drink made for a festive occasion. I thought about calling my friend Otieno. He would have loved it but I was here on business. We could always come back another time.

"It's about the Pharmacist who was offed in his garage," I tried to lead the way.

"Yeah, the Indian fellow, Mehta, they charged his wife, no?" he replied, looking at me, his eyes searching.

"I'm working on the story," I said and sipped on my drink.

"Yeah…" he said as he cleared his throat, waiting for me to tell him exactly what I wanted him to tell me.

"There seems to be something fishy about the whole thing – it's like she is being set up," I ventured.

"And you know this how?" he replied.

"Well, I don't know for sure but something stinks."

"Let me see, you have a hunch," he said, half – smiling. "And what is it exactly that you would like me to do?"

"Well, I visited his pharmacy and the manager, an American woman, was very evasive – it's like she was holding something back. I wanted to know if you would maybe look into it, you know, a little deeper."

He broke out into another bout of hearty laughter.

"Too much TV is not good for you! Those American shows, eh? *CSI Miami* or is it *Law and Order*? That's not how it works here, you know. Look. An arrest has been made and the suspect was charged, but you are suggesting that somehow, someone planted evidence to incriminate her, on the basis of the evasive looks of a white woman? Wow!"

I felt a little silly but I did not want to sound needy by pressing the matter. He had left the door open and that was good enough for the time being. So I thanked him for the beer and stood up to leave.

"Hey, stick around and meet my new partner, Special Agent Njoki. She'll be here any minute. You won't regret it."

I looked at the time. It was still early but I did not want to wait – we had said enough to each other.

"Next time, man, next time," I said as I walked out.

I decided to stop by the New London Grill. I had not seen Meredith in a while and although we had a date for Saturday, I felt compelled to see her this evening. I walked in and sat at my usual table but instead of Meredith, another waitress came to take my order. I contemplated having another beer but I hated drinking by myself so I asked for iced tea instead.

When, Ben, the manager, informed me that Meredith was not in, I decided to just leave – what would be the point of hanging around? So I left my iced tea intact, not happy to have paid for it, and walked to the bus station where I boarded a commuter bus, *Ladies Choice,* to Dagoretti.

I had recently moved to a new rental property, complete with a working gate, a permanent security guard and neighborhood watch – three levels of security that made the area that had seen its fair share of violence feel safer. The rent was a little bit more than what I was paying at my old apartment but it was a nice trade – off: a little less money in my pocket but a little more sound sleep at night.

I sunk down on the couch and turned on the TV to catch on the day's happenings. The lead story was about a woman who had just returned home from Saudi Arabia, where she had gone to work as a domestic worker but found herself serving more than she had bargained for. As she narrated her ordeal, in an exclusive interview with Citizen TV, my mind wandered back to the Mehtas and shortly after that I drifted off to sleep.

Chapter Five

I was just about to enter my office the next morning when my cell phone rang. A voice I did not recognize, scruffy but with a slightly European accent was on the other side.

"Jack Chidi, I am made to understand that you are interested in a certain case, yes?"

"Who is this?"

"I just don't think it's a good idea," he went on. "It's never a good thing asking too many questions, don't you think?"

I stopped, looked around me and then moved to the corner of the building, not too far from the security officers who manned our building.

"Yeah, who is this? And what questions are you talking about?"

"Take care!" he warned. "And by the way, you look good the way you are. Try and stay that way."

Click. I looked across the street for anyone with a cell phone, then at the cars parked or driving by. It seemed like everyone was minding their own business. I ran inside the building and straight to Bulldog's office.

The more I tried to explain it to him, the more it sounded incredible. Bulldog was staring at his computer with a disinterested look on his face. He then looked at me as if to see if I was done and said:

"I don't know why anyone would threaten you."

"It does not make sense to me either."

"You say the only place you have been is the pharmacy?"

"In a way, yes, but I did meet with Mrs. Mehta's defense lawyers at Nova; and with Dube at the Corner House; my last stop was at the London Grill, but I hardly talked to anybody there."

"Well, I think you and Oticno need to look into that pharmacy again and see what is going on there: partners, suppliers, clients, and employees – the works. And oh, yes, take Jacob with you."

Jacob was the company driver and he knew his way around Nairobi like one who had an internal GPS.

As I walked out Bulldog's office, I had a queasy feeling, an unsettling sensation in the pit of my stomach. It was not fear, it was something else; something that I only experienced when I was getting closer to what I was seeking and with that the knowledge of how exposed I was. It came with an awareness of my own vulnerability, which is what always kept me sharp and focused.

When I met up with Otieno and Jacob, I gave them an update. Otieno volunteered to use his sources to sniff out Mehta's business connections. I did not have a good plan of action but I knew that I would have to start from the beginning. I also called Dipti – I needed more than she had given me about the Mehta's. I asked if we could meet and again she agreed without raising any objections.

We met at the Six Eighty Hotel, this time just she and I. She was wearing another business suit but it did not look odd this time around. We ordered some coffee and as soon as it came, I told her, in no uncertain terms, that if I was going to work with her at any level, she would have to tell me all she knew about Vishal Mehta – everything! We had focused on Mrs. Mehtas case the first time we met but now I needed everything she had on him, on his wife and on their daughter, Saranya – all of it!

She looked at me for a second and said, "Fair enough, and I will ask you to let me know as soon as you uncover anything, anything at all, no matter how small or insignificant."

She sipped on her coffee, cleared her throat and then placed her elbows on the table. Her face softened for a moment and became somber as she started to tell me about the Mehta family.

Vishal Mehta was born in India and migrated to Kenya soon after his tenth birthday at the behest of an aunt who owned a retail store in Kiambu. He attended the Aga Khan Academy, and then left for India to attend Puna University in northwestern India – the Oxford of the East, as it was popularly known.

After his graduation with a degree in Economics, he returned to stay with his aunt and found work at a local bank, first as a teller for several years, eventually rising to be branch manager. His marriage to Anarupa, arranged by his aunt, came shortly after. Promises of a family soon evaporated when Anarupa was diagnosed with ovarian cancer and had to have her ovaries removed. They moved back to India and after two years they came back with a daughter – Saranya.

Vishal went back to work at the bank but a robbery almost cost his life. It certainly cost him his job. Whether freely or forced, he left the bank and opened up a small pharmacy on Muindi Mbingu Street.

"Why forced?" I interrupted.

"Well, you know how it is. There was some talk of him being the inside man on the bank job," she said in a neutral tone.

"Did the police look into it?"

"I don't recall," she said and paused.

"But you feel like there was something shady…"

"I can't say. But all I know is that he focused his energies and time on his business venture – establishing good relations with doctors in the major hospitals in and around the city who in turn sent their patients to his pharmacy."

"For a kick back," I added but she continued without pause.

"You see, despite his mild – mannered nature, Mehta knew how to pull the ropes by whatever means necessary: gifts, lunches, dinner parties, paid vacations and cold hard cash. In a country where cash is king, the currency holder is the…" she left that for me to finish.

"King – maker," I said with a smile.

"But now you see, such arrangements never end well. There is always one side that sooner or later demands more than the other is willing to concede and thus a business partnership that starts out well usually ends in a mess…"

"Are you suggesting a motive?"

"No, no, I'm just throwing angles at you."

"But you do not think Mrs. Mehta is…"

"I just know that my client was not involved," she said and paused.

I looked out of the window, trying to digest all that she had said.

"What about the girl?" I asked.

"Saranya…well, typical Indian girl, too much into music, went to Loreto Convent Msongari. She actually surprised me when she said she wanted to become a teacher to work with underserved school districts – like Kangemi. She seems quite reserved."

"Would she do it?"

"Do what? Kill her father? Ha! Come on now Jack, really?"

"People do crazy shit all the time."

"Where would she even start? They were very close, her

father and her. He adored her and I'm sure she felt the same."

"I had to ask."

"I know. Anyway, she was asleep – her mother can attest to that. Can you imagine waking up to your mother's screams and finding your father slaughtered in his garage?" Dipti asked.

"Whoever did it did not care, that's for sure. But tell me this, why did he move his business from Muindi Mbingu – not a bad location really – to Parklands?"

"Well, the business outgrew the capacity of the premises and so they decided to move Mehta Drug Emporium to new offices with more square – footage."

Dipti did not have anything else on the man but she dwelt on the manner of his death: multiple stab wounds in the chest, which had punctured his lungs and then severed an aortic artery. Whoever had killed him had done it with extreme prejudice. He had died painfully – and slowly and there was no way, she said, her voice rising to the occasion that her client could have done that. She loved him and she was a woman who could hardly hurt a fly, let alone a doting husband of many years.

"Who were the silent partners?" I asked.

"Well, I don't know them but I think they have an international branch or international investors – one or the other but I guess any pharmacy would have that kind of connection."

"Doesn't she know any of them?" I asked.

"Mrs. Mehta does not seem to know too much about the business. In this day and age – can you believe it?"

I couldn't agree with her more.

Chapter Six

Saturday morning. I woke up with an erection. It was not unusual but this one was noticeably taut, almost angry. I pushed down on my penis to quiet the angst but it pushed back. I quickly jumped into the shower and the cold water calmed things down quickly.

I was expecting Meredith. I had planned a full day of activities with her but the phone threat had changed my plans for outdoor ventures.

"Are you sure you want to watch movies all day?" she had asked.

I did not know how to say it without alarming her unnecessarily by telling her that I did not want to drag her into harm's way or that I would not be able to enjoy a romantic outing with danger hovering over us.

"It's your company I am more interested in," I said playfully, and added, "Moreover, I figure no restaurant in town can beat my eggplant parmesan, with a spring salad drenched in balsamic and olive oil vinaigrette."

"Aah, fancy! Are you reading from a recipe book?" she laughed but she had not objected.

I ate a hurried breakfast and begun to clean up the apartment. I usually kept a clean house, thanks to my mother who had instilled in me a sense of cleanliness as I grew up. I did a good job at it but every now and then I would slack off a little bit, especially when I was working long and crazy hours. But one thing I never ever did was to leave the house before making my bed. I don't know when that habit formed but it was one I had taken to like a duck to water.

"It makes life easier when you keep things in order," my mother always said to me.

"Cleanliness is next to godliness," I would blurt out wryly.

"No, it just makes sense, being organized; it gives your life order."

She would then smile as she always did when she imparted these tidbits of wisdom to me.

I did not have much to do in terms of cleaning – just some dirty clothes that I had piled up in the corner of my bedroom that needed a wash; the pile of pots and pans and two plates that needed some serious scrubbing and the cabinets and shelves that demanded some dusting.

It did not take me long to get my place ready. I then quickly ran out to the shops to get the items I needed for lunch. I did not want to spend too much time out in the open but I was not going to starve my date either because of fear. A kilo of goat meat, some wine, cheese, a midsize eggplant and cilantro in my basket, I then headed back.

I was about to cross the main thoroughfare cutting through Dagoretti Corner when a car came burrowing down from my right. I jumped back and fell, spilling my groceries all around me. The car zoomed past me, raising a cloud of dust. It was a black Mitsubishi but I was unable to catch the number plate. I waited, watching the dust settle slowly and then I stood up, dusted myself off and gathered my groceries.

I was not the only pedestrian to have jumped out of the way. Others now emerged from the bushes yelling obscenities at the runaway vehicle.

"Damn these Indians! Why do they let children drive? He can't even see where he is going!" a woman standing by the kiosk yelled out after the car.

She insisted she had seen a child behind the wheel of the offending Mitsubishi. I might not have been the intended target but I was not taking anything for granted – I hurried to the safety of my home.

I looked at myself in the mirror and that's when I got really mad at the goddamn driver – my carefully selected clothes were all muddied up. I looked at my watch. Meredith would be here any minute and so I had to move quickly to make myself presentable. As I took off my muddy clothes, I caught sight of myself in the mirror again. I noticed I was losing some of the weight I had gained over the years. My work in the gym was beginning to pay off. Not that I was overweight but, back in the day, I used to be chiseled and I was trying to reclaim my lost form.

Boxing had been my life and getting back to it, while not an easy thing, had brought another level of joy. Any boxer will tell you that there is nothing like connecting with two left hooks to the body of your opponent and finishing with a right cross to the head. Boxing is an art form that requires dexterity, good hand – eye coordination and, if you are lucky, hand speed. But if you were anything like me, you compensated your lack of speed with head fakes and a high work load – which simply meant you overwhelmed your opponent from the first bell until they surrendered – or fell!

I jumped in the shower and washed up quickly. Then I put on a pair of jeans, a white T – shirt and made it to the living room. There, I pulled out my collection of CDs. As Lionel Ritchie begun crooning from the Panasonic surround system I had purchased years ago, I walked off to the kitchen. I needed to start preparing lunch before Meredith got here.

I had just pulled the eggplant parmesan from the oven

when I heard a knock on the door. I turned the volume on the stereo down and walked to get the door, taking a last glance around the apartment to make sure everything was where it needed to be. I pulled the door open and there she was. She smiled, softly and invitingly. I gave her a hug and she wrapped her arms around me – gently at first then gave me a squeeze before she pulled herself away.

She wore a long beige skirt that hugged her nicely around the waist. I thought her top, a sleeveless cream shirt with a small pink ribbon just above her left breast, made her arms look longer. She had a small scar on her neck that showed above a beaded necklace with matching earrings. I closed the door behind me as she kicked off her shoes and made herself comfortable.

We had not said a single word. I walked in behind her as she took a quick tour of my abode, not wanting to break the silence. There was not much to see really but she took her time going over the framed photos of my childhood. She then moved to the one on the TV stand: my mother, looking straight on as if in deep thought.

"That's my mother," I whispered, my first words.

"I know," she said, smiling. "She looks sad, yet so strong, this woman," she added, as she picked the framed photo up and ran her fingers over it.

I had never seen Meredith so radiant and alive.

I went back to the kitchen to get started. She came in behind me and asked me if she could help. I looked at her for a minute then decided that she could help with the salad while I worked on the pasta that would go with the eggplant parmesan.

"So, you cook a lot?" she asked chopping the lettuce.

"I try, but it's not easy when it's just me."

"If you cook like this I can visit more often."

"Let's see how you like the taste first."

She laughed. It came easy, the smiles and the laughter. It forced her cheeks to push against her cheekbones, thus making her face look rounder, youthful and charming.

After lunch we sat down on the sofa and I poured some wine. I had seen all the movies in my collection so I asked her to make a choice. She opted for just talking and, with the music playing on, the afternoon rolled into evening.

We talked. We danced. We laughed. And then we kissed.

It was a soft kiss – tender, probing, unsure. Her eyes held mine; searching with softness that only need can conjure. Then we kissed harder and deeper, each reaching for something that only the other one could give. I heard the sound of my heartbeat, like drums from a time gone by, faster and faster. Warmth washed over my body. I allowed myself to melt in it, the drums eased into a silence that was only interrupted by heavy breathing. The world outside faded into an autumn of darkness. And we slept.

We woke up early enough the next morning, showered and had some breakfast – eggs and toast. She had a few errands she wanted to run before her evening shift at the London Grill. We did not talk much, which can be a good thing sometimes, but I did not want her to leave just yet.

After we cleaned the dishes, she picked up her bag and I walked her out.

"I really had a good time last night, Jack," she said when we got to the bus station. "It's been a while since I felt that way with someone," she added softly, as if re – living the highlights of the evening.

"That's why you should stay," I said.

"Next time, lover boy," she said and playfully jabbed me in the ribs with her index finger.

She boarded the bus. I waited until it was out of sight then hurriedly walked back home. I sat on the couch where Meredith and I had shared some moments. A faint trace of her perfume still lingered. A smile cut across my lips as my mind started replaying my night with her. But it was not long before I felt lonely – and almost sad.

I had thoroughly enjoyed her company but now guilt crept in. I had not told her about the speeding car or the telephone threat. I was putting her in danger by having her around me, just like I had once done when I was investigating the City Murders. It was best, I thought, to tell her the truth and let her make a decision on whether she wanted to stay with me or not, instead of keeping her in ignorance.

The phone interrupted my guilt trip and the slide into loneliness. I picked it up expectantly but it was only Otieno calling.

"Hey, what's up, Otieno?" I greeted, hiding my disappointment.

"Are you alone?" he asked.

"Yeah, man. She left not too long ago."

I heard him let out a little laugh and I knew what was coming next.

"How was she? I mean, now that camel days are over…" He broke off, screaming gleefully.

"Man, what do you want?" I asked, trying to get him off my back.

"Tell me more. Describe those pointed breasts, man."

Otieno was a good guy to hang out with but he was like a bloodhound, sniffing out details, especially when it came to women and sex. He was a married man with three children but he acted, at times, like a bachelor on the prowl. And it got him in more trouble than it was worth.

Like the time he was making out with some girl in a bar – she was married and the husband walked in on them. He was irate and charged at them. But Otieno, grinning from cheek to cheek admitted loudly to his transgressions, claiming that she had told him that her husband had a small dick and that he did not know what to do with it either.

The husband, a well – built mechanic with a reputation for being violent, his manhood questioned in front of strangers, decided the proof was in the pudding. He pulled down his pants and paraded naked in front of the patrons. Everybody cheered him on, and burst out laughing. He had forgotten that it was a cold night. So when he looked down, and for a second, he could not see his dick, he forgot about Otieno and ran out – embarrassed and humiliated.

"Did you call this early to probe my private life?" I asked.

"You can't keep this from me, man. I tell you everything. But anyway, now that you are back to earth from amorous clouds, I have something for you. I think I've found our mystery silent partner…."

"Who?"

"Did you not hear me? Mehta's silent partner, eh?"

"Who is it?" I was now all ears.

"Jakuma Mohali."

"Jakuma who?" I asked, not sure I had heard right.

"Mohali, the former Kenyan Ambassador to the United States."

"Are you sure?" How did you find him?"

"Discreet inquiries and you know that I have my contacts," he retorted, his voice resonating with his signature grin. "I Googled him, not much there, but here's the kicker: apart from being an avid supporter of President Joakim, Mohali was not known to be amongst the wealthiest cats in town – that was before he was appointed financial attaché in the New York Office of the Permanent Mission of the Republic of Kenya to the United Nations."

"Was he the guy who...?"

"Dude, listen. One year into his new job, he was recalled, quietly and given a less visible position in the Immigration Office, where he worked for five years before going into private business. And almost overnight, he became a self – made millionaire."

"Do we know what kind of business he has, apart from being a partner at MDE?" I asked.

Otieno smacked his lips before answering me.

"Yes!" he almost shouted, "Some illegal shit!"

We both broke out in laughter – but we knew that his words had an echo of truth riding with them – the same could be said of many instant millionaires in the country.

"So what else do we know about Mohali?" I asked.

"A huge appetite for booze and women – all kinds of women – he does not distinguish between married, single, young or old."

Booze. Women. A sleaze – ball, for sure, but that had nothing to do with the pharmacy or Mehta, unless they were seeing the same woman.

It had to be something else, something huge. Perhaps MDE was not doing as well as they had anticipated before the move and they had quarreled over some money. Could it be that Mehta owed him a favor that was never returned? Buggers like Mohali always collected on debts owed, no matter how small or how large.

I stood up from the couch and walked to my desk for my notebook.

"Good deal, man," I complemented Otieno. "There was another guy – William…"

"Not yet. But I say we shake Mohali and see what he knows about Mehta's death. It's an angle worth pursuing." He sounded happy with himself.

Chapter Seven

Monday morning, Jacob was waiting for me outside the gate in the company car – a late model Toyota Pajero. We drove the short distance to Otieno's apartment. Akinyi, his wife, met us at the door and ushered us in – he was not ready yet, she told us. But that he would be out shortly. She offered us some breakfast – coffee, eggs and toast. We sat in the living room, cluttered with children's toys and clothing.

Jacob was looking around the room – it was his first time in Otieno's home and perhaps he was trying to reconcile what he had imagined it would be like to the mess that we were wading in. I smiled at him but he did not reciprocate. I finished eating my eggs and just then Otieno walked in hurriedly, tucking his shirt into his pants. He then hooked his corduroy jacket with his index finger and twirled it over his shoulder with hubris and walked towards the kitchen.

"What's up fellas?" he greeted cheerfully, his grin as wide as ever. He leaned over to Akinyi and planted a wet one noisily on her lips. She pushed him off gently.

"We have guests," she said, protesting the public display of affection but I could tell she did not mind at all.

He smacked her behind playfully and walked over to where we were and sat down, looking at Akinyi to bring him his breakfast. She ignored him and continued washing dishes. He smiled at us and then cleared his throat – suggesting that she was forgetting something. She gave him one look and continued with the dishes. He gave up and walked over to make himself a plate.

Once Otieno gulped down the last of his toast and eggs, he gave Akinyi a goodbye kiss – he never left home without a kiss except on those days when she was pissed off at him. We thanked her for the breakfast as we walked out, jumped into the car and drove off.

Jacob, as usual, looked quite content driving. Last time we rode together, he had proved to be quite resourceful with his knowledge of the city and the surrounding metropolis – and with his skills behind the wheel.

Mohali's office was in a nondescript office I had never noticed before, near the Kenyatta International Conference Center. We walked into a quiet and empty lobby save for the front desk clerk, a small man with boyish looks who was talking on the phone. To my question about Mohali's exact office floor, he pointed in the direction of the elevators, breathed out "eleventh floor" and continued his bored interlocution. I did not bother to thank him.

The elevator doors opened to a quiet long corridor on both sides. To the right, about ten meters away, two big men in black suits stood facing us. We walked towards them and I explained that I needed to speak with Jakuma Mohali.

"Do you have an appointment?" one of them asked.

"No, not really, but it's important. My name is Jack Chidi and this is my partner, Otieno Kibogoye. We are with the *Daily Grind*."

I pulled out my ID card and handed it to the man who had spoken. His buddy stood quietly by, his eyes darting from me to Otieno and back again. He was chewing on a toothpick that he moved from one side of his mouth to the other.

"Wait here," the man with our IDs said and walked through the doors.

We stood there with Mr. Toothpick who now put on an unnecessary grin on his face. I looked at Otieno and smiled at him and then at Mr. Toothpick who mistook our friendly gesture to be a signal of sorts. He opened his jacket, and slipped his right hand in. I knew what that meant and I was not about to test him.

Just then his partner appeared with our IDs.

"You do not have an appointment," he said, his tone having changed to a more belligerent one.

"I already told you that," I said irritably but firmly. "We will just take a minute of his time."

They looked at each other and then moved up and stood right in front of us, daring us to make a move. Before we could react, two girls walked out of the office holding some paper documents. Reading from their faces as they walked past us, they were excited about something, the documents perhaps. They called the elevator. Otieno pulled my hand and together we jumped into the elevator with the girls, making it seem as if it was the attraction to the girls rather than the bullies' stare that made us move on. But knowing Otieno, this was an opportunity to get to know the girls.

They were quiet but their faces still showed elation. One of them wore a black skirt, black shoes and a white top and a brown purse hanging from her right shoulder – she looked like she was in school uniform. The other one had blue jeans, sandals and a white T – shirt that hugged her tightly around her chest.

"What are you two so happy about?" Otieno asked, grinning from ear to ear.

He was eyeing the taller of the two, the one in jeans and then he looked at me and winked, signaling that I should play interference. I was not up to it but I started to say something and then I changed my mind. I had more important things to think about so I turned and looked at the floor numbers decrease as we descended. Try as he could, Otieno did not get anywhere with them. As we stepped out of the elevator, the two girls walked past us with him still trying to get them to say something.

I tried to imagine what Mohali or someone in his office had told them to make them so vibrant.

Eventually, I decided to try to call his number.

"M International, good morning, how may I help you today?" a pleasant voice answered. I imagined she was as pretty as her voice.

"Hello. My name is Jack Chidi with the *Daily Grind*. I would like to have a word with Mr. Mohali."

"Weren't you here just now?" she asked, dropping her cheerful voice altogether.

"Yes, I was but I did not get a chance to explain the nature of my business…"

"You have to make an appointment."

"Is he available anytime today?"

"No, he will be out of the country for a few days, but you can make an appointment for another time if you like."

"When does he come back?" I asked, irritably.

"Sir, do you want to make an appointment, yes or no?"

"Hey, listen. I am trying to…"

She hung up.

Otieno suggested that instead of returning to the office empty – handed, we pay a visit to the Pharmacy and snoop around.

"You think we might be lucky?" I asked absent – mindedly.

I had not made any progress with the white woman during the first visit there, but that did not mean that we would strike out again.

"Sometimes it is better to be lucky than good," Otieno said, making me wonder what he meant, but I did not object to his suggestion.

The drive to Parklands was not bad in spite of the mid – morning traffic and when we pulled in, Jacob strategically backed into a parking spot at the far end of the lot so that we faced the entrance. There was not much happening, just a few customers driving in and out for their prescriptions or whatever. We hunkered down and waited.

"So, Jack, how was it with Meredith?" Otieno started off.

I knew it was just a matter of time before he asked to hear all the details of my evening and night with the delectable Meredith.

"Oh come on, man, we just had dinner and talked," I answered, adding: "She is really good company."

"Did you get some? That's all I want to know."

I was not about to discuss my night with Meredith – I did not want him undressing her in his imagination. But he was persistent.

"That's just wrong, man," he protested. "You know, if it were me, I would tell you everything!"

"Another time, man," I answered, looking around as if to remind him that we were on a job.

There was not much activity going on – just a stream of walk – ins and drive – ins – women with small children, old men with walkers and their wives in tow. There was nothing that stood out of the ordinary – just another day at the pharmacy. We had wasted half a day chasing dead end leads – and yet a lot of activities surrounding Mehta's death whirled around me – the phone call that came after my first visit there, the car burrowing down the road and only narrowly missing me, the security guards at Mohali's office. But how did all these tie to the murder?

Yet I was convinced that whatever we were looking for was not far off though we had very little to go by. I was about to call our snooping a dud when Jacob started fidgeting in his driver's seat. I followed his gaze. He was looking at two girls walking towards the pharmacy. Just as they went in through the doors, I recognized them: they were the same two we had seen at Mohali's office earlier on.

What were they doing here? Perhaps Mohali had set them up with jobs; after all he was a partner. There was just one way to find out: someone had to run in and listen to whatever was being said. Otieno would spook them and I had already shown my face once at the pharmacy. So it had to be Jacob. He raised no objection to that. It was Otieno who protested but I silenced him with a look that brooked no argument.

Jacob jumped out and walked into the pharmacy. I asked Otieno to sink back to his seat. Just then, a black Audi pulled up to the front door of the pharmacy and three men jumped out. It looked like they were in a hurry. Jacob was still in and I was not sure how he was going to handle himself if there was trouble. I looked at Otieno but he seemed unconcerned.

"Should we go in?" I had to ask.

"No, man, just wait, I think he will be okay."

We did not have to worry after all. Jacob came out with some papers of sorts. He got in the car and handed me the fliers. It was a listing of allergy warnings for Synthroid.

"I told the pharmacist that my mother was having a kind of reaction to her thyroid medication and I wanted a list of possible side effects so I would know what to look out for."

I smiled. That was quick thinking!

"The two girls were called in to the back office by a white woman. I did not get what they wanted or why they were there but it was certainly not to fill a prescription."

"What about the three guys who come in?" Otieno asked, sounding a little tense.

I turned to look at him. His eyes were intense and he immediately pointed towards the door.

"Hey, look!" he called out.

The three men came outside and stood by the Audi. Shortly after, the two girls also came out, hugged the men. One of the girls, the one in jeans, got in the car with the men and drove off as the other girl, the one with the school – girl looks, slowly waved at the car as it sped off. Then she started walking towards the bus station. I was not sure if we should follow her or the Audi. We decided to split up. Otieno and Jacob would follow the car and I would follow the girl. I rummaged through the seats and glove compartment and found a brown cap that I hurriedly put over my head, low, to provide some disguise.

The girl walked across the street to the bus stop and waited for public transportation. I pulled the hat lower to cover my face and walked to the bus stop. I stood several feet behind her.

A *matatu* came and she inched forward to get in. I followed, allowing three or four people in front of me before I clambered in. I found a seat two rows behind her. Then I looked around me, trying to memorize the faces, clothing and any suspicious behavior from our fellow travelers. After the phone threats and car incident, I had to assume that I was being followed as well.

Her stop came quickly and I had to scramble to get to the door before the *matatu* took off again. Several passengers were pushing to come in as I exited.

Outside, an old woman was struggling to lift her food basket to her back so I helped her with it. She stumbled a little bit once the full weight of her load was on her back but she found her footing and was well on her way without a word of thanks. But my attention was elsewhere. The delay had given the girl a head start, but I caught a glimpse of her just as she disappeared round the bend.

I ran to the corner and as soon as I had her in my sights, I slowed down and just followed at a safe distance. We turned off the main road and after about half a mile, she turned towards a cluster of residential housing. I crossed the road, keeping close to the kiosks and makeshift eateries.

After a few yards, she walked up a narrow driveway and opened the gate to a two – storied house. Then she stopped to fumble into her bag for house keys, opened the door and walked in. Should I follow her into the house and ask her what her business was with Mohali and the pharmacy? It was a fleeting fancy. Why would she even talk to me? I walked past the driveway to the end of the street, made a right turn and walked into the first fish and chips joint I came to. There, I ordered lunch – a plate of homemade fries and pork sausage.

I called Otieno. I needed an update before I decided on the best course of action.

"Where are you guys?" I asked.

"We are in Lavington – they drove into this bungalow, really nice house. We are waiting to see if anyone comes out but so far there has been no activity. What about you?"

I told him that the girl had gone into a house and that I presumed it was where she lived. I gave them directions to where I was and asked them to find me there.

I did not have to wait long for them. They pulled up and I jumped in. They had not had lunch so we went to a small Indian Restaurant off Ngara road. We walked in and a waiter, a young man, ushered as to our seats. He then gave us huge menus covered with red plastic that felt greasy to the touch. He left to bring us water while Jacob and Otieno flipped through the menu for lunch specials. I pushed mine aside and wiped my hands with a napkin.

Otieno ordered Lamb Masala and a Kingfisher while Jacob went for Chicken Tikka. I only asked for tea.

"How come you are not getting some food, man? Did Meredith put you on a diet already?" Otieno asked, laughing out loud at his own joke.

"Come on, man, I just had some lunch. But I could always use a bite off your plate if you insist."

He gave me the eye, smiled and did not say another word about food.

Although I was not hungry, I was salivating from the aromas emanating from behind the beaded entrance of the kitchen. I looked around at the décor. Various depictions of Vishnu, Brahma and Shiva graced the walls. Soft Indian music played from invisible speakers.

Suddenly, a loud commotion interrupted the music and made me jump. It was the restaurant manager, an Indian with a huge belly, leading the way. He was admonishing one of his workers. He had some choice words that included the worker's mother and a small mouse.

"Get the fuck out! I fire you right now!"

The worker, a young black man, got out of the kitchen and gave the Manager the middle finger.

"You know where to put it!" he shouted indignantly.

"Yeah, get out, you bum! Go suck your mother's tits!"

"Give me my money, you bugger, before I tear this whole place up!"

The Manager paused, then rushed to the tiller and pulled out some notes, folded them together and threw them at the young man, who now smiled, picked up his pay and walked out, mumbling something about flies in the curry goat.

This incident reminded me that I needed to check on all of Mehta's employees – past and present. A disgruntled employee might have had it in for him, you just never knew.

The waiter brought out the food and Otieno forgot about the commotion as he dug in. I took that opportunity, amidst the din, to think of the best way forward. The girl was a link between Mohali, the Pharmacy and Mehta. We had to go and see her.

After lunch, I gave Jacob directions to the house. It was only a few blocks away and soon we pulled up outside the gate.

I rang the doorbell and then rapped on the door. She had to be in there somewhere and we would not budge till she showed up.

The door opened and the girl looked at me, then at Otieno and then at Jacob who was manning the gate. She then looked at Otieno and me again.

"I remember you two," she said as comprehension dawned on her. "Did you follow me home?"

"No, we got information on you from the pharmacy," I replied. "Can we come in?"

I flashed my badge but she did not seem to care much about it. So I handed it to her and she stared at it as I did the introductions.

"My name is Jack Chidi with the *Daily Grind* and this is my partner, Otieno. That over there is Jacob, our bodyguard."

I added that bit to bring in a sense of urgency to the matter. She then looked at my badge and handed it back to me. She looked confused – lost, really.

"May we come in?" I added. "We just want to have a word with you. It's important."

She looked at us again – studying our faces, and then opened the door wider and we walked in.

She did not offer us a place to sit so we just stood there in her living room.

"We are not here to cause you any trouble," I started off, all the while looking into her eyes. "We are investigating something bad that happened to someone we know. We are hoping that you can help us. No, no…you are not in trouble yourself."

I added that on sensing that my words had made her even more uncomfortable, almost alarmed.

"We just want to know the nature of your visit to Mohali – like why you and your friend went there today."

"I don't know if I'm supposed to talk to anyone about this," she started and then hesitated.

From her voice I could tell that she was really scared.

"I promise you that we will not tell anyone," I reassured her.

Her shoulders dropped.

"We were just looking for work," she said resignedly.

"What kind of work?" Otieno asked.

"Just domestic work, sometimes they offer to send girls…" she started to say but did not finish.

Just then, we heard a loud screeching sound and car doors banging shut. Jacob came half – running into the house and locked the door behind him.

"What is it?" I asked, turning around sharply.

"Looks like trouble," he said, trying to stay calm.

I ran to the window, pulled the curtains and looked out. I saw the gate shake and then open violently and two men came running towards the house. I recognized them. They were the same ones Jacob and Otieno had tailed to a bungalow in Lavington. Somehow, they had turned the tables on us.

"Oh shit! We've got to get the fuck out of here. Is there a way out at the back?" I whispered to the girl, realizing that I had not even asked her name.

She just stared at me – frightened and confused, perhaps wondering if we were part of a planned robbery.

I was about to plead with her when we heard a loud bang at the door. It sounded like gunfire. The girl screamed, and fell to the floor. I followed suit and crawled behind a couch. They rammed the door again.

She pointed to the kitchen. Otieno, without as much as a word, took off, followed closely by Jacob.

I jumped up from behind the couch, grabbed the screaming girl and pulled her behind me as we ran out through the kitchen and out through the backdoor.

We found ourselves in a small unfenced yard that ran into the back of some apartments. We ducked under clothing lines and ran as fast as we could into an alleyway that pilled out onto Ngara Road. Then we waded through the thickening lunchtime traffic and lost ourselves in the crowds.

A few blocks down the road, we walked into a coffee shop and that's when I realized that I was still holding onto the girl. I let her hand go and apologized – trying to massage her wrist but she pushed my hand away.

"Are you injured?" I asked her.

"No."

She rubbed her hands together. I asked her to sit down. I could tell she was undecided but she sat down anyway – the narrow escape may have created a bond, and I quickly sat next to her. We all peered into the street through the large window hoping that we had lost the attackers.

We were safe – for now.

But we needed to get away from Ngara as quickly as possible. There was only one place to go – Kiambu. Perhaps Solomon would house us for a while. I called him while Otieno corralled a cab.

We asked the cab – driver to drop us off at Machakos Bus Terminus where we ducked between buses and the throngs of travelers, just to confuse any would – be pursuers. It would have made sense to take the cab all the way but I was not sure that we had enough fare for a long taxi – ride. Besides, no one in their right mind would shoot at us in the crowd and with police patrolling the terminus.

We boarded a Kiambu – bound bus and took the rear seats. We were among the last few to board and we were now well on our way.

As we rode to Kiambu, I wondered about the girl. She had stuck with us thus far. Was it out of fear of us or of them? Who was she? What was she to them?

"I will explain as much as I can when we get there," I whispered to her.

"What the hell is going on?" she asked. "Who were those people?"

Her voice was trembling and I could see her lips twitch.

"They have something to do with a case we are investigating, as I will explain later," I repeated.

I knew that she too had some answers to some questions and perhaps when she told us all she knew, we might be able to piece together a narrative that made sense. But would it tie into Mehta's murder?

As the bus chugged along, my mind drifted back to Meredith. I liked her a lot and although we had not spoken since, I could hear her voice whispering into my ear, or smell her soft skin against mine if I closed my eyes long enough to allow myself to dream.

But the reality of the present broke into my dream. I now looked at the girl sitting quietly between Otieno and me. Jacob was one seat behind us. She still looked confused and terrified and I felt bad for her.

To allay her fears I said, "Hey, don't you worry, we will keep you safe."

"Safe?" she looked at me incredulously. "After someone was trying to kill us and you are talking about being safe?"

"We did not know that they had followed us."

"Exactly! You brought them to my door and now you want me to trust…?"

Clearly she had no clue that the same guys who had driven her friend were the ones who had just attacked us. I would keep it that way.

"Look, once we get to Kiambu, you can go your own way – perhaps there is someone you can call. But I would rather you came with us – we can help each other out."

She clasped her fingers together and placed them on her thighs. She did not look my way.

We alighted at the Kiambu – Limuru Road intersection and walked over to the Red Nova. Solomon would meet us there. I asked Joe for a private room in the back and he had just the place we needed – an office in the back where he kept the band's musical instruments and also where they rehearsed.

It was a large room with two long couches and several arm chairs lining the walls.

"Who is this most beautiful lady?" Joe asked, cheekily.

"My name is Lidia." She took Joe's extended hand.

"What can I get for you to drink?" Joe asked, still looking at Lidia. "Are you guy's hungry?"

"I could use some water," she said, pulling her eyes away from his gaze.

Otieno asked for cold beers for the three of us. "Lidia, that's a nice name," Otieno stated. "I'm sorry that all this craziness is happening. That is why we need you to tell us all you know about the people you are dealing with."

She looked around the room as if she was contemplating an escape and then asked, "Who were those guys chasing you and why were they after you?"

"Those are Mohali's men," I answered.

She looked at Otieno and then turned to me.

"Why would he send men after you?"

"That is what we don't know. We just wanted to ask him a few questions regarding a case we are working on. Something does not quite add up."

"What is your association with M International if you don't mind me asking?" I said to her.

"It's just a job. I... we were interviewed for a job but I did not get in – well, I have to check tomorrow to see if my papers came through. That's all. But what case is this that you are investigating?"

"Your papers...what papers?"

Before she could answer, Joe came in with the drinks. She took her water, gulped it down quickly and handed the glass back to Joe.

"You sure you don't want something stronger, beautiful?" he asked, smiling broadly. She did not answer. We thanked him for the drinks and he left.

"Please, continue. What papers?"

She fidgeted in her seat and then told us how she had come to Mohali. She had just graduated from Ngara Secondary School. She was looking for work but nothing was coming her way. She remembered that at school she had come across some pamphlets about an agency that hired baby sitters and house – helps to work either locally and abroad.

"The papers said that you could work part – time even while in school and make hundreds of dollars in income. The literature claimed that all that was needed was someone who wanted to work with kids, a willingness to travel abroad as needed and at least a two year commitment to the agency."

She had called the number on the pamphlet and she was given an appointment and that's when she met Azani.

"Azani?"

"Yes, the other girl. We met at Mohali's."

They had filled out application forms, the usual: names, address, parents, siblings, family income and other identifiers. They were promised that once they got past this initial stage, they would be called for interviews – and if that worked out, they would be assigned mentors to help them before they were placed.

"And how much did you pay for all these?" I asked skeptically.

"Nothing, they pay all your expenses and they also give you a stipend. That is what I was collecting today at the pharmacy – my friend was placed."

"Where did they place your friend?" Otieno asked, sounding more levelheaded.

"She is going to America together with some other girls. They are so lucky."

She sounded disappointed.

"How come you did not qualify?" I asked.

"My visa was not processed in time but I got a stipend anyway. I was supposed to check back tomorrow for the next available overseas assignment."

"Are there any domestic appointments?"

"Yes, but I don't want to be placed locally," she said contemptuously. "I want to see the world."

I was still trying to get a handle on it when Joe came bustling in with more drinks – followed closely by Solomon.

"Hey, Jack, you sounded serious on the phone. Is everything okay, son?"

"Yes, now that you are here!" I answered as we shook hands.

Over drinks, I tried to explain what I knew thus far – from Mehta's murder, and now this. The more I talked, the more

I realized that I did not have much. I did not know how all these connected and how this led us back to Mehta. The only thing that joined them together, at least on paper was that Mohali had invested in MDE, where his recruits went to get their stipends and other travel prerequisites.

"So you guys think there is something sinister with these recruitments?" Lidia asked.

"That's what we are trying to find out."

"I know several girls who went and came back with lots of money."

"Honestly, Lidia, I don't know exactly how this is playing out but I can assure you that we will get to the bottom of it – one way or the other."

She looked at me for a brief second.

"I really need this job, you know." she said.

"I know all this sounds crazy, Lidia, but don't you worry." I tried to sound confident but I was getting confused by the minute.

Under cover of darkness and several beers later, we drove to Solomon's house. For now, we just needed some good night's rest, or what was left of the night.

Chapter Eight

I woke up to the sounds and smell of breakfast. Solomon had risen a little early to prepare something for us to eat. I joined him in the kitchen after my shower. I felt rested despite the short night. Solomon was wearing a robe that seemed to wrap around him twice. For someone who had done so well for himself, he had remained humble and skinny – a trait that for many seemed to disappear with wealth.

"Morning, Jack, I hope you are hungry," he said as I poured myself a cup of coffee.

"Do you always get up this early to make breakfast?" I let out a huge yawn and stretched out my back.

"My mother always said that breakfast is the most important meal of the day." He laughed as he flipped an egg omelet on the pan with expert hands. I sipped on my coffee.

"So who is this girl, really?" he asked, almost in a whisper.

I walked to the kitchen island table, pulled a bar stool and sat down facing him. I did not know much about her so there was nothing to tell. I figured today we would get in touch with her parents or whoever she was staying with to let them know that she was safe and sound. In the meanwhile we needed to know why M International was getting so hostile.

Solomon looked at me and said, "I met Mohali once."

"Really?"

"Yeah, at the American Consulate: a party thrown in his honor. Crazy guy got drunk and became quite obnoxious. You should have seen how he was acting, just plain stupid and aggressive with the women, it was embarrassing!"

"Do you guys know each other?"

"Not really, why?"

"I was hoping you'd get us inside."

"I can ask around if you want."

"Yeah, man! If we can just have a word with him, we might be able to get to the bottom of this shit."

He plated an omelet and slid it towards me, "How about that?" he said with a smile. I took a bite and I had to confess he was not a bad cook – sautéed green Zucchini, aged sharp cheddar and organic eggs.

Otieno, Jacob and Lidia were still sleeping. I smiled thinking of the early bird as I chased a piece of omelet with my tongue.

I had phone calls to make so I excused myself after breakfast. Solomon offered me his office located a few doors down the hallway.

I first called Detective Felix Dube and told him about M International and about the break – in at Lidia's house. I gave him the address. Then I called Bulldog to say that we would not be coming in that morning. I did not mention anything about abandoning the company car.

I went back to the kitchen. Otieno was now hungrily eating breakfast and trying desperately to convince Akinyi on the phone that he was not with another woman. He then hang up and looked up.

"Hey, where's Jacob?" Otieno asked between two huge bites of his omelet.

"And what about the girl, Lidia?" I added.

Solomon volunteered to wake them up. I took another cup of coffee and sat down next to Otieno. His face, stuffed with an omelet, did not show the exasperation of someone who had just had a fight with his wife.

Jacob was the first of the late sleepers to come in. He was in his boxers. Otieno and I looked at each other and then back at him. His knees stuck out like bony planks that seemed to move in a circular motion with each step.

I was about to ask him to put some pants on when Solomon came running in and announced that Lidia was missing. We all stood up and ran about the house calling out her name but she as nowhere to be found. She must have left as soon as we had all gone to sleep.

Something tightened inside me. I called Felix and told him that the girl was gone. He was quiet but I could hear him breathe. After a little, while he cleared his throat.

"Okay, Jack, I will check it out," he volunteered. "But we should get one thing straight: I am in charge. You follow my lead or you are out. If this is what I think it is, someone is going to get hurt. I cannot have bodies all over my city. Remember last time, eh?"

He seemed to be bringing up the City Murders case every time we spoke and it was getting annoying. It was not my fault that so many people had died – in fact I was pretty sure that had it not been for me, many more would have died.

I paused, thinking carefully before I gave an answer. He did not need to remind me of the past.

"We are on the same page – you handle your end and I will handle mine."

He hung up without conceding another word.

What a baby! I don't know what was with him and a sense of entitlement. I tried not to take it personally, but there was a part of me that felt slighted: like he expected me to play second fiddle for the rest of my life.

I pulled out Mehta's business card to get the address for Solomon. He had volunteered to go into the pharmacy, under the guise of doing business, and see what he could gather. I handed it to him and he looked it over.

"Yeah, I know where this is. I used to have some business out that way, if you know what I mean." He smiled knowingly.

Otieno jumped on that opening.

"Say, man, where are those girls you had at the party?"

Solomon laughed again, shaking his head and said, "Man, you know how it is with me and the ladies – they come and go, nothing too serious, nothing permanent."

I had to get them back on track.

"Solomon, do you think you can give us a ride to town?"

"Sure, unless you guys want to borrow the Toyota. I would not mind really – and since you are coming back this way anyway, it might be better if you have transportation."

He had a point. We took the Toyota and headed towards Lidia's. I prayed that she had not tried to get back to the same house. My senses heightened, and everything around me seemed different. I don't know why but everything I valued in an otherwise mundane existence became petty. I looked for a constant, for something to make the present look real again, like Otieno's perpetual grin – but the grin on his face was gone. No one in the car said a word.

We turned on to Ngara Road and into some thick traffic. We almost came to a standstill as we turned onto the street leading to Lidia's house. No one in the car said a word. Jacob, at the wheel, his face beading with perspiration, let out a huge sigh and I quickly followed suit. I tried some quick breathing techniques but I forgot the count and found myself hyperventilating.

"Hey! Stop! You can't go in there. Turn around!"

It was a policeman, banging on the hood of our car.

Jacob pulled over and rolled down his window.

"What's going on, officer?"

"There is a house – fire up front. Pull in there and turn around," he said pointing at a small field by the side of the road.

We jumped out and ran towards the burning house. Otieno, though in worse shape than I, managed to keep up with us as we scurried and pushed through a crowd that was gathering and increasing by the second.

The house was completely burned down. The fire brigade had recovered what appeared to be human remains but they were so badly charred that they could not be identified. A partially burnt ID card recovered on the body was the only identifier. Lidia was gone.

Chapter Nine

Felix Dube was talking on the phone when I spotted him. I pushed my way through and once he finished with his call, I tapped him on the shoulder.

"Can we talk?"

"Hey, Jack, follow me."

We walked briskly past the cordoned off area and before long we were sitting in the back of his police cruiser.

"Here's the deal, Jack," he started without much ceremony, "It's possible that we are now dealing with a homicide unless the girl committed suicide. It will take time to identify her but I need to shut this thing down quickly."

I was not sure if he was asking me for help or he was merely thinking out loud. I studied him – his face, stoic and almost serious but with a playfulness that could be mistaken for complacency. I could tell he wanted me to throw him a bone – give him something that he did not have but was too proud to ask for directly.

I felt myself choke up, thinking of Lidia but I managed to keep it together.

"She has a friend," I told him. "They were hired by M International for some overseas assignment. It's only that hers did not go through – she was going to check back in today."

"Yeah, yeah, I know, I know," he said rather hastily.

"I know where that other girl might be," I added.

"Yeah, I meant to ask you if she had mentioned where the other girl was." He was looking straight ahead at the commotion in front of us and then he turned to look at me.

"I need names, Jack. I'm not going to have bodies all over my city."

It was a silent order. I took a deep breath and let it out slowly.

I started to tell him that I was just as concerned about the loss of life but that is not what came out.

"I am getting a little tired of your threats, Felix," I growled. "Fed up with verbal or physical threats coming at me from the bad guys and the good guys, my editor included. I'm tempted to write what I know right now and let the chips fall where they may."

We stared at each other – each trying to wrestle for an up over the other. There was no hatred, at least not the kind that tears people apart – just the will to remain autonomous and in control. I could tell that he was a little taken aback and he tried to cover it up by staring harder at me.

Then he broke the stalemate with a thin smile that seemed to offer some understanding. I acknowledged that concession with a nod.

"We will take you to her," I told him after a little while.

Felix did not object. He got on his phone while I walked back to Otieno. Jacob had taken advantage of the police presence to see if the company car was still where he had left it but it was nowhere to be found. He looked distraught but I told him that once we got a police report, all would be well.

We jumped into Solomon's Toyota and with Felix Dube and his partner, a female under – cover agent named Njoki. She wore grayish black pants that fitted her well despite their used look. Her hair was cropped into a small afro which suited her. She had a freshly vibrant face but her forehead, furrowed by time belied the youthful vivacity.

We headed out for Lavington where we hoped to find Azani before she disappeared into the blue.

We drove all the way in silence. I looked out of the window as we whisked by elegant mansions, fronted by smooth lawns, cast – iron gates and sidewalks complete with uniformed nannies walking their charges in strollers and leashes. At the Valley Arcade shopping center, we stopped to regroup.

"Let's get several things in order," Felix started.

We were all standing outside, huddled like a team of rugby players, listening to the coach.

"I need you guys to stay in the car when we get there. I will do all the talking – all of it. No questions. Are we clear?"

He did not wait for an answer. He walked back to his car, followed by Njoki. And just like that, Felix was in charge again.

We drove up Gitanga Road and after passing a few homes Jacob slowed down and parked the Toyota to the side. Felix and Njoki pulled up beside us and Jacob pointed to a driveway a few meters ahead of us. Felix nodded and started driving up and then stopped. I was not sure why he was stopping. He got out of the car and walked back to us and asked me to join him, leaving Otieno and Jacob out in the street as our back up.

At the door, a middle – aged white man with an athletic build greeted us. His freckled face had a hard look to it but years of practicing how to belong had softened it – just enough to smooth the edges. I knew guys like this in the ring; they came at you – textbook stuff. But as soon as you landed a few to the body, they forgot about the book and the street fighter in them came out roaring at you.

"What's up man?" he greeted, his arms outstretched.

For a minute I thought that he and Felix knew each other. But it was the greeting that caught Felix off guard.

"Hi there!" he answered, awkwardly.

They shook hands.

"Come in, come in," he invited us with a huge smile.

He patted me on the shoulder patronizingly as I walked past him. I caught a whiff of alcohol in his breath. He then looked at Njoki, eyeing her the way someone eyes a shirt they might consider buying for a relative but were not quite sold to it yet. Horny white bugger, I thought to myself.

We walked in to the living room. On the wall was a framed photo of a tearful President Obama at his inauguration. Right next to it was a photograph of his grandmother, Sarah Obama, standing in front of a wooden house that looked like it was built in a hurry. Felix walked to the far end of the room and I followed.

The furniture was simple; crafted lounge chairs with cushions made from African print and an imitation Ghanaian *kente* cloth, a bamboo coffee table. To the left was the kitchen – stainless steel refrigerator, microwave, double stacked baking oven and a wine – rack curved into the wall. Glass cabinets holding china that seemed to reflect the light coming from the glass sliding doors that led to the pool surrounded the dining table on the other side.

"Can I get you something to drink? We can sit here or we can go to the game – room."

He did not wait for an answer but walked through the living room, slowing down long enough to look behind him to make sure that we were in tow. He pushed a button on the wall, and smiled as the wall opened to display a pool table, a full bar, and a movie theater.

He went straight to the bar and poured himself a stiff one. Felix followed suit. Hell, I was not going to be left out so I joined in. Only Njoki abstained. She walked around the room. I had not heard her utter one word and Felix had not bothered to say more about her, which told me that they were or had been intimate at one point or other.

"So what can I do for you?" the man asked as soon as we had our drinks.

"Well, Mohali sent us to discuss…"

"Uh, bastard should have just called."

"Not over the phone."

"Ah, yes of course. You guys are good," our host was saying to no one in particular. "But don't get me wrong, I am so glad that we are moving them quickly, eh?"

He elbowed Felix and laughed. Felix joined him. He was playing along and doing a good job at it. I walked over to the pool table and ran my fingers across the felt. I took the triangular ball rack from the wall, laid it down on the table and then pulled the balls from the pockets.

"Do you mind?" I asked, as an afterthought.

I had allowed myself to get comfortable.

"No, please help yourself, eh? You play good?" our host asked and then laughed out loud like one who was drunk.

He then lit a cigarette, sucked long on it and let a bellow of smoke from his nostrils. He reminded me of some arrogant white dude I had hustled some years ago but I did not say a word.

"So where are we now?" Felix asked.

He had jumped right into character without breaking a sweat.

"If she is good we can get her out ASAP. America seems to be eating them up!" He laughed out again, as he eyed

Njoki. His eyes now told me that he had been drinking for a while.

He walked over to a desk standing at a corner and pulled out a folder, opened it up and scrolled down with his finger as if looking for something.

"The others are gone already?" Felix asked, casually and without hesitation, like someone who really knew what they were talking about.

The white man laughed again; that throaty laughter of self – assured competence, before he said, "Oh, yeah, the other ones were gobbled up but not before I had a good taste, eh?"

He let out that sheepish laughter again. The 'animal' in me begun to rise but I held it in check, trying to stay away from it all – just like Felix had requested.

I pulled a cue stick from the wall, chalked up and slid it back and forth, between the index finger and thumb of my left hand. I bent down and placed the cue under my chin, my left hand giving anchor and with one smooth move, I pulled it back and crack! The balls went flying across the table, clanking each other until the violence of the break quieted down and each ball rolled to stake its own claim on the felt.

I had hardly had time to admire the break when I caught Otieno at the entrance with the corner of my eye. He was violently pushed into the room like a rag doll and then Jacob came sprawling to the floor right behind him. Two men followed, guns drawn. I turned around to face them and placed the cue stick on the table. Njoki was at the other end of the room and the two men had not seen her.

"What is this?" the white man asked, putting his drink down.

"We found them at the gate. They are the same ones who have been snooping around."

"Who are you?" the white man, coming off his high, asked, looking at Felix.

He reached into his desk drawer and I assumed he was going for a gun. Felix, with a move that astounded me, was on him before he could pull the drawer open. With the same motion he pulled his gun from his shoulder holster and let out two shots towards the entrance.

One of the guards fell.

The other guard, not sure if he should return fire for fear of hitting his boss, aimed at Otieno and Jacob. I heard one single shot and I saw him slump forward before he collapsed into a heap on the floor. Njoki had shot him.

The white man took that momentary lull to clock Felix with a huge right cross to his jaw that Felix never saw coming. I saw him begin to hit the floor and just then I heard one more shot and I saw the white man spring backwards, a spray of his blood hit the wall behind him as he fell to his knees, clutching his right shoulder. I saw Njoki take aim again and shoot. The bullet hit the wall behind the white man and just above his head. That was just a warning. The next one was not going to miss.

"Ok, ok, ok! Don't shoot. Don't shoot!" The white man, now ashen, was shaking visibly.

He tried to raise his hands up and only managed to move his left hand. Njoki was on him, gun trained to his head. She cuffed his hands behind him and went to tend to Felix who was now coming to.

"You don't know who you are fucking with," the white man managed to say between the pained laughter he was sputtering out arrogantly. "You are all dead!"

She slapped him with a backhand and he fell to his side, curling himself into a fetal position. He was quiet for a minute and then started spewing obscenities and threats to call the Navy Seals. Njoki walked over to him and kicked him hard in the ribs. He now understood that he was no longer Mr. Boss – man.

I was still holding the pool stick in my hand like a javelin when Njoki looked at me and asked if I was planning on doing anything with it. It was the first time I had heard her speak and the first time I was taking a good look at her. She helped Felix to his feet. Otieno and Jacob were still on the floor, their hands covering their heads, when she asked them to stand up and take post by the door.

"Call for back up!" Felix ordered after he had massaged his jaw back to function. Njoki reloaded her gun before she dialed a number on her cell phone. She then went to the door and relieved Otieno and Jacob off guard duty.

Felix walked over to the white man, knelt next to him and whispered something to him. He then pulled him to his feet and asked me to bring him a chair. Felix pulled out his badge and showed it to the white man. He froze.

"What is your name?" Felix asked calmly.

He placed his hand on the white man's shoulder and looked him straight in the eye. For a split second I thought he was setting up to punch the daylights out of him.

"My name is Roger Caldwell. I am an American citizen, and a businessman. What do you want from me?"

"What kind of business are you engaged in – Mr. Cordell?" asked Felix, pulling the syllables of the name, making it sound comical.

"It's Caldwell. I am a contractor – a middle man if you will."

"Tell me about the girl, Mr. Cordell."

"My name is Caldwell…not Cordell."

"I'll call you whatever I want!" snarled Felix.

Roger looked around, as if weighting his options. When he finally spoke, he uttered the most unusual of requests on Kenyan soil.

"I want a lawyer."

We burst out laughing, not at the absurdity of it but at the way he was holding on to American jurisprudence. Felix reminded him that he was not under arrest and that if he cooperated, he might even let him go. We all knew that unless the man had more guards coming to his rescue, he was done for.

"In a few minutes this place will be crawling with cops. We are going to go through everything in here with a fine toothcomb. I am sure we will find something that will put you away in a Kenyan prison for a long time. So please, tell me about the girls."

"I ain't telling you motherfuckers shit. I am an American. You can't do shit to me!"

Felix managed to smile a little. He leaned over to Roger. People who remain calm under strenuous circumstances, or smile at great insult scare me. They scare me because they use that same nerve and calculated demeanor to put a hurting on you.

Felix did not show anger or impatience but his tone had dropped just a tad.

"You surprise and disappoint me at the same time; I am asking you a simple thing; tell me all you know or I will find it some other way, with or without you."

I was not sure why the American was not getting the message. Sooner or later, he was going to talk.

I walked over to the desk in the corner where he had been standing and picked up the folder that Roger had been perusing. It was a ledger of sorts, not detailed but it had contacts. I did not see anything of importance, just overseas phone numbers and a listing of countries – Saudi Arabia, USA, and Britain, Philippines, Brazil and several others.

I turned the page and a small card slipped out and fell to the floor. I picked it up. It was a business card; William Burrows, Managing Director of Logic Placements. There was a phone number and an address in Texas. I flipped the card over – there were some writings that I could not make out, underneath it was a name: Azani Mutiso – Texas, Wagio, Jane – Japan and some dollar signs next to their names.

William Burrows! Was this our man? It had to be the William Mrs. Mehta had mentioned, the other business partner.

Felix was still trying to get some information from Roger who was now defiantly insulting his intelligence. It is one thing to insult Felix Dube by calling him names but it was another to try to belittle him and then laugh in his face.

"Mr. Cordell, I am giving you one more chance to start talking."

"Hey, Roger, who is William Burrows?" I asked. He looked up at me and snarled, so I asked him again. This time he spat in my direction.

Felix placed his hands on Roger's shoulders and then walked behind him and un – cuffed him. Roger rubbed his wrists together and then placed his hands on the sides of his thighs – he did not get up.

Felix pulled his gun from his holster, checked his clip for bullets and then placed it back in its holster. If Roger knew what was in his best interest, he had better start talking, I thought to myself, or reach for his piece.

"You have three seconds," Felix said and started the countdown. He did not get to two.

Roger spat in his face and said, "You are full of shit, you black mo…" Just as he started the insult, his left hand reached for a small firearm tucked in his boots. He raised it up but before he could fire, Felix shot him once between the eyes.

*****

The next day I went to Felix to ask what they were going to do about the American connection. If these guys are sending women abroad, then we need to know where and why. These guys might have been the ones who killed Mehta. It was the logical step, it seemed to me.

"We don't have enough to get Interpol involved. This is an international…" I did not let him finish.

"So you are not going to pursue these buggers all the way to the States?"

"No, Jack, that will take a lot of resources, paper work, jurisdiction and most of all it will need proof that we do not have to justify it. Even if we had something tangible, something that ties this to an international organization, we would still have to go through Interpol."

I don't know what I said to him but he could clearly read disappointment on my face.

"This is not a story, Jack, these are real criminals with dangerous intentions as you have already witnessed. But anything that crosses borders and nations needs careful groundwork. We shall of course do what we can to find out the facts – and then see where that leads us, yes?"

I did not answer.

After I left Dube I went to the office. Bulldog and I needed to have along, long talk. I was tired of this whole thing.

I think he knew I was coming and I let him have it – all of it. Even with my voice quivering and at times loud and angry, one thing that remained constant was his demeanor – that nonchalant – poker – face he had cultivated through the years – whereas I rattled on and on about my findings.

And even after I was done, all I remember seeing was his smug smile – a smile that did not quite hide his curiosity but one that offered me nothing to work with.

But I was also determined.

"I want to go to Texas, dig around and see what I can come up with… I have an address, the office of Logic Placements. I also have a friend, you remember Irene Kizito…"

"Yes, yes. Of course the brother was killed during the City Murders, right?"

"We have to find the girl, Azani Mutiso and then William Burrows. Somewhere between these two is the missing link to Mehta's murder."

He sat back on his chair and looked at me without saying a word.

"Well, okay. Just be careful and keep me updated." With that he sat up and logged onto his computer as I walked out. "And Jack, bring all the receipts."

That was his notion of accountability – and it was not all monetary.

Two days later, I was on a plane to Texas.

Chapter Ten

Houston, Texas, was nothing like Nairobi. The warm humidity hugged you like a blanket as soon as you stepped outside the air – conditioned George Bush International Airport. The languid smell of concrete and asphalt that hang in the air was palpable.

Irene Kizito was waiting for me. I had sent her an email as soon as Bulldog authorized my request to follow the story to the United States and she had agreed to house me. It was going to be a busy week – but having someone who knows the place to show me around was a comfort.

"How was the flight?" she asked.

She looked beautiful, even with a little perspiration forming on her upper lip.

"Long, really long but I tried to sleep as much as I could."

"You did not have one of those talkative flight – mates, did you?"

"Thankfully not, but I had a window seat and there is nothing as boring as staring at the darkness outside. I don't know how Armstrong did it, all the way to the moon and back."

She smiled as we drove off.

"We are now on Interstate 45, headed west," she said, after we had driven a little while. "Downtown," she added, noting my eyes on the heavy traffic that had slowed us down.

"It sure does beat Nairobi," I added.

She cast a glance my way and asked, "It's getting better though, right?"

"Not yet but we will get there – slowly but surely."

The traffic crawled on and then opened up.

"How is the family?"

She hesitated before answering.

"Well, the children live with their father now. We are separated – divorced really – always hated the D – word."

"Oh, I'm sorry, I did not know…"

"Don't be. It's better this way, for the kids. I see them on some weekends."

I was not sure if I should ask her what happened and so I left it alone.

"So, tell me again what brings you here. You did not say too much in your email so I figured it had to be top secret."

"If I tell you I might have to…"

"To kill me?" she finished. "That is so lame."

I agreed with her and we both laughed.

"It is my first visit to the Lone Star State," I said my thought loudly. "Apart from the number of people wearing hats and string ties, it's just like any other major American city I have seen on TV in Kenya: congested roads, big buildings, big banks, pizza parlors…"

"…tanning beds, gun shops complete with shooting galleries and bad attitudes," she cut in.

We laughed again.

"But remember," she added quickly, "there's more to a place than the stereotype. Take Nairobi for instance – Nairobbery?"

She had a point.

She looked good for one who had gone through so much in such a short time and I admired her for it. Why would any man want to leave her?

She interrupted my thoughts.

"Here we are."

She stopped the car to activate the gate, a metal arm stretching across the drive. The arm rose up like a soldier giving a stiff salute and we drove through. She then made a left and she pulled into a thin driveway as she activated the garage door opener. The garage was really narrow so she pulled in slowly to avoid running into something. I looked at her, craning her neck to see the front. I smiled but she was focused on the task at hand. After she put the car in park, she closed the garage door behind us. We got out and walked into the house.

It was a modestly furnished two – bedroom apartment; a beige couch and sofa, a small coffee table in a cozy living room complete with a fireplace. She had a flat screen TV mounted to the wall above the mantle and some framed Kenyan paintings on the sidewalls.

On the other side of the room, sliding glass doors took you out to the patio and small yard where she said she planted her own herbs and an assortment of greens. The kitchen was separated from the living room by a long counter, which made the whole space look bigger than it really was.

"Let me show you to your room."

She started walking upstairs and I followed. I had brought a small bag with me – my Dictaphone, some clothes, two pairs of shoes and some personal effects.

"I know you said you don't have much time but why don't you freshen up and then take a nap while I get dinner ready?"

She pulled the door behind her and I jumped in the shower.

It was just what I needed. For once it was good to take a nice long shower without worrying of water running out in the middle of your bath. After the shower, I lay down on the bed and tried to take a quick nap. I was too wired to sleep but I forced myself to rest for a little while.

Irene had dinner waiting for me when I finally made it downstairs. She had prepared some rice, beef stew and a salad. Over dinner, I told her why and what had brought me to Texas.

I had to find Azani. To do that I had to go through William Burrows and Logic Placements first so as to find out what exactly was going on. If it turned out that they were a legitimate placement agency, then we were back to the drawing board – with Mehta's killer still at large. But it was worth a shot – it was the only one we had.

"From what you have told me, I know you don't think there is anything legitimate about all these."

It was more of a question than a statement and I had to think for a suitable answer. So I took a bite of the salad in order to buy sometime.

"It is one of those things where you hope to find a resolution quickly but you are also scared at what you might find," I finally said.

Irene sipped on some wine and then said, "If they are exporting drugs using the women as mules, they are not going to let someone just come in and disrupt their operation."

She looked serious; as if she was trying to warn me to be careful without saying it. I smiled at her and added that I was always careful.

She was right about drugs. And it was another angle to look into. Drugs and drug trafficking had become quite an issue in Kenya lately. Rumor had it that some newly minted millionaires were involved but no major drug kingpin had been busted, yet.

After dinner we watched a little bit of TV before I turned in. Tomorrow would be a busy day.

*****

I woke up to the rays of the sun streaming into the room through the corners of the curtains adorning the bay window. I squinted, trying to get my eyes oriented to these unfamiliar surroundings – the corner computer desk, the mahogany dresser and the brown leather seat in an otherwise quietly understated room.

I placed my head back on the pillow and closed my eyes. But there was no more sleep left in me – it was time to get to work.

After a quick wash, I dressed up and walked downstairs. Irene was reading the *Dallas Morning News* which she now placed on the seat next to her as she stood up to greet me. She was wearing a ted T-shirt and a pair of shorts.

"Hey, there he is. You look rested."

She hugged me. I put my arms around her gently at first and then with a little more pull to it before we let go.

"Good morning, Irene. You look good," I said without thinking.

"So do you!" she answered.

She smiled as she turned and walked to the kitchen to get me some coffee. My eyes followed her, profiling a youthful energy in her step. I swallowed. I felt that deep hollowness one feels when they long for something they couldn't have. I turned and looked away, trying to think of Meredith but my eyes slowly went back to Irene, who was now walking back towards me holding a cup of Joe.

"So, what do you have planned for the day?" she asked as she placed the cup in front of me.

She did not have any make up on – not even lipstick. Her hair, braided into three mounds on her head, looked like three door knobs – but she still looked beautiful.

"I just need to find the offices of Logic Placements."

I fumbled for the business card and gave it to her. She looked at it for a second and then handed it back to me.

"That's downtown. You can ride with me in about an hour – I have a work meeting. Or if you want you can take the bus. It'll drop you right into the central business district. You can't miss it."

With a straight face I said, "I'll just take a *matatu*."

She looked at me for a second and then burst out laughing, her shoulders rocking like pistons. As she walked past me she rubbed her hand across my shoulders. I could hear her still laughing as she went upstairs to get ready for work. I went to the patio to get some fresh air and finish my coffee.

After Irene left for her meeting, I decided to make some phone calls. First, to Otieno and after he teased me about using company resources to travel abroad to meet a woman, he got back to business. They were tailing the white woman who worked at the pharmacy but nothing had really come out of it. He promised to call me back if anything happened on that end.

I was about to call Felix but I remembered the conversation we had before I left and I let it go. I'd call him later when I had something to tell him.

I made it by bus to the Houston CBD at about two o'clock that afternoon. I hailed a cab. When one stopped to pick me, I jumped in. The driver, a youngish – looking white man with a sing – song accent, which I later learned was the southern drawl, stepped on it as soon as I gave him the address.

"What brings you to H – town?" he asked after he had established that I was visiting from Kenya.

"Just the usual tour, to see the world," I said, hoping that the non – committal answer would let him in on the fact that I was not in the talking mood.

"I hear you. I've seen a little bit of the world myself," he said with a chuckle and then shook his head. "I was in Iraq and then Afghanistan – did three tours."

"Wow. That's quite something," I said.

"Yes, it is, man, yes it is!" He was still shaking his head. "But tell me; how is it over there in Africa? My friend Gus is always trying to get us to visit. I hear y'all crazy as hell!" he said, with a laugh that did not sound contrived or mean – spirited.

"You heard right, we crazy as hell," I rejoined. He looked at me through the driving mirror and found that I was smiling.

"Oh shit, we all fucking crazy – that's for damn sure! How long will you be in town?"

"Not long. Just enough to get a feel of the place, you know?"

"Yeah, man, you need to experience real Texas, real America – big food, big drinks and I likes some big women."

He laughed again, heartily. I looked at him again and thought to myself that, without even trying, I had found an American Otieno. But there was something else in his eyes – coldness I had only seen in guys whose lives had seen thorny patches – and lots of them. My cousin Mburu had had such eyes.

"Tell you what," he started, "When I finish my shift, I'll take you around, show you the life, eh?"

I know a hustle when I hear one but this one was not even new; it happened all the time all over the world – a scamming taxi cab driver taking unsuspecting tourist for a ride – figuratively and literally.

I contained my irritation. As long as I was aware that he was trying to hustle me, I could turn it to my advantage.

"Cool!" I answered calmly.

It did not take long after that to get to my destination. I paid him and stepped out of the cab.

"Call me, man. I'll show you how we do it in the Lone Star State," he sung as he handed me his business card, "Name's Dale." He pointed to his card again as if he was asking me to confirm his name – so I did.

"I'm Chidi."

He cocked his head to his side and asked, "Who?"

"Chidi."

"Chi, who? Hell, man, you got yourself a nickname or something?" He chuckled and continued, "I'm sorry man, but what kind of name is that?"

"Just call me Jack."

I did not have time to fool around with him. I'd save this for another time. I was intrigued at how quickly he had given up on my name.

"Yeah, I like that – Jack. Anyhow, just call me and I'll take you to some girls, real big Texan women, but don't get me wrong man, they ain't hookers or nothing man, just big old good gals having a good time."

Logic Placements was housed on the fourth floor of a modern building across the street where Dale had dropped me off. I walked in and decided to take the stairs – for exercise that I was not getting too much of lately.

I made it to the fourth floor effortlessly, which surprised me a little. I opened the stairwell door and found myself at the far end of the building. I started walking down the corridor. Ahead of me, a door opened and a woman walked out. She took a few paces and stopped, then pushed the button to call the elevator. I heard a ding, followed by the sliding doors of the elevator and she took two steps and disappeared into the wall.

I walked past the elevators and the next door down the corridor, where the woman had appeared from, was the office of Logic Placements. I paused for a second, looked up and down the corridor and then extended my hand and knocked. There was no answer. I waited a few seconds before knocking again. I waited for a few more minutes and then I took the handle and pushed the door: it was locked. I shook the handle again, trying to push it open – nothing!

I turned around quickly and ran to the elevators and pressed the call button. It was still on the first floor. I ran down the corridor and took the stairwell. I had to catch her before she disappeared into the crowds.

Once on the street I looked both ways to see if I could catch a glimpse of her but she was nowhere to be found – and amongst all the white faces milling around me I realized that I would never be able to tell her apart for the next white woman I saw – they all looked alike to me!

I looked at the time. It was almost three and while she could have been going out for a late lunch, it was also possible that she was gone for the day. I called the number on the card and it went straight to voicemail. Well, there was just one thing to do: get some food and a drink and wait to come back later on.

I was getting a little flustered. I knew I did not have much time but there was nothing I could do about that. Once word of Roger Caldwell's death at the hands of the police finally made it to his partners, whoever and wherever they were, the trail was going to get cold quickly.

I walked into Big Bertha's Steakhouse and was met at the door by the hostess, a young African – American woman. It felt good to see another black person in this sea of whiteness. I said a huge hello and followed her as she led me to a corner table. She set the huge menu she was holding in her hands in front of me and told me that a waiter would be with me shortly.

I had hardly made myself comfortable when my waitress came to take my order. She was holding a pitcher of ice – cold water in her right hand. After she filled up my glass she proceeded to give me the special for the day. I listened and after she was done, I asked for a Budweiser and some chicken wings to start.

"Mild or hot?"

"Mild."

"I'll be right back with your order, Mister," she sang to me with a drawl I had often heard in old spaghetti westerns.

"Thank you ma'am," I answered.

My mother had always told me that it was a good rule of thumb to be nice to people who handled your food – advice I once ignored with very dire consequences.

I looked around me. There was a couple in matching cowboy outfits dancing on what looked more like a boxing ring than a dance floor. The music, some bluegrass with high octane beats had them synchronized, turning this way and that way before they came together for a little shimmy and followed by high kicks that had the whole restaurant clapping in glee. Soon, other couples joined in the festivities and before long, the whole ring was a carnival of cowboys and cowgirls twirling and yodeling.

"Here you go, honey."

It was my waitress with the wings and drink. She placed them in front of me and pulled out her writing pad from her apron. She had a tattoo of a snake coiled around an apple tree. She was not bad looking but she was nowhere near Eve.

"Are you ready to order, sweetie?" She asked before I could thank her.

"Yes, please. Let me get the T – bone steak, medium rare, a side of broccoli and corn on the cob."

"Excellent choice, honey, excellent choice!" she said without a smile.

She turned and left as I sipped on my beer. It was nice and cold. I then went to work on the mild wings – not half bad! After I was done, I turned my attention back to the dance floor. The last time I danced was with Meredith in my apartment – I was going to call her as soon as I got back home.

A loud clutter brought me back from my reverie. It was the waitress with my order. She was balancing a huge tray with her left hand from which she pulled out a bottle of A1 sauce and some hot sauce.

"Here you go, baby," she said.

I thanked her with a huge smile and pulled the steak towards me. I pushed all the condiments away; a good steak never needs dressing. I took a bite, savoring the juices that shot out of the medium rare steak. The taste, soft and exquisite, brought floodgates of memories of those days at Anne's Butchery in Dagoretti – I was home again.

After my late lunch, I went back to the Logic Placements office but there was still no one there. I would have to wait until tomorrow. I thought about going back to Irene's but that meant being alone in the house watching TV. Hell, I was better off going back to Bertha's – at least they had music and beer – I might as well enjoy the sights and sounds of the Lone Star State.

I asked for another Budweiser as soon as I walked in and took a seat at the bar. I then reached into my pockets and pulled out Dale's business card and dialed the number. He was happy to hear from me and said that he was on the way to drop off the cab and would be with me within the hour.

I wondered if Irene would join me for a drink after she left work but I thought the better of it. Perhaps I could ask her out tomorrow night.

Dale joined me almost three drinks later. He sat down noisily and ordered a Texan burrito and a St. Arnold. He looked at my empty bottle of Budweiser and shook his head before asking the waitress to bring me a St. Arnold as well.

"You in Texas now, man!" he said and smiled at my protestation.

His shift was now over and he was ready to party and he let out that loud "Yeehaw!" I had been hearing all evening. Texans and hollering go together, I mused to myself, just like *nyama choma* and Tusker.

"You like cars, Jack?" he asked.

"Yes, well, not particularly."

I was not sure where he was going with this and it was not something I had given much thought to.

"You guys ain't got no Nascar?" he asked almost shocked.

He pointed around the décor of Big Bertha's: posters of race cars with their drivers and crew showering each other with champagne.

"We have the Safari rally – very popular…" I started to explain but he cut me short.

"Ain't nothing like it, man, the roar of the engines, the speed, the booze and the women…"

He looked haggard for someone who was no more than thirty years old at best. His arms, which showed signs of having been strong once, were covered with a velvety blondish – red hair which reminded me more of those caterpillars I used to see back home just after the rainy season.

I did not ask him much about himself and I was not going to. I knew he had seen combat in Iraq and Afghanistan but that was the extent of it. The less we knew about each other, the better – but I needed him to trust me enough to be my guide as I navigated Texas looking for Azani and William.

"So what's the plan, ma man," he started just as his burrito made it to the table. He rubbed his hands together before grabbing it in his once massive hands and taking a huge bite. Some of it escaped from the sides of his mouth and slowly found its way back on the plate. I sipped on my St. Arnold.

"I need a little help with something. It was something I thought I could do by myself but, obviously I underestimated the level of difficulty, seeing that I know no one here." I looked at him but he was more interested in the burrito. "It might be a little involving but please don't feel obligated. I just thought I would ask."

"Man, I got your back, man. This is Texas!" He took another huge bite.

"I am looking for my sister. She was brought here by some folk who might not have her best interest at heart, if you know what I mean."

He stopped in mid – bite, the burrito suspended between us.

"Whoa! Hold on up there, cowboy. What you mean?"

He leaned forward before placing his burrito back on the plate.

I feared he was going to say no to me but it was worth the try.

"Say that for me one more time," he requested.

So I repeated what I had just told him. He sat back in his chair and looked at me without saying a word. I guess he was trying to figure me out. He then picked up his burrito and so I continued.

"I would really love to go to the police but I have nothing concrete – just my word – hardly enough to convince the law to help."

"Yeah, you need more than that to get the Texas Rangers excited," he chuckled.

"I have an idea where she might be, or rather I know who might have her and all I want is to take her back home, no fight, and no fuss."

Dale looked at me for a second and then took a small bite and then another one. He chewed nosily and I could see he was deep in thought – perhaps wondering whether to trust me or not.

"Well, what do you need me to do?" he asked, looking at me expectantly. "I can get some of my boys – but that will cost you."

"I would rather we do this quiet," I answered. "It can get ugly quick and the last thing we need is to have too many players."

He nodded in agreement but his eyes had that register of concern so I continued.

"I don't have much money to pay you but I will make it worth your while. After all, what I need is a ride later on and if I need to get away in a hurry, I need to know I have someone waiting."

"You are going to break in, aren't you?"

I did not answer. I waited for him to work on his burrito and his drink instead. The waitress came by and I paid up just as he was finishing up. He was a fast, uninhabited eater – just like most Kenyans are.

"You like?" Dale asked after we had stepped onto the sidewalk.

"Yeah, that was good eating," I responded rubbing my stomach.

"No, I mean do you like her?"

He was pointing to a red Ford Mustang that was parked right in front.

"She's a beauty ain't she?" he asked with a voice that sounded more like singing.

He did not wait for me to answer. He walked over and opened the door and got in. I followed, and as soon as I sat down, he started the engine. It sounded like those rally cars that used to zoom past us in Limuru, leaving us covered in dust or mud, depending on the season.

Dale looked excited. He revved the engine twice – looking at all the different gauges mounted on the dashboard. He then put it in gear and floored it. For a few seconds all I could hear was the squealing tires as we peeled off and joined the traffic heading back towards the CBD and then we were back to crawling – so much for a sports car in the middle of evening traffic.

A few minutes later, we were outside the offices of Logic Placements. We walked upstairs down the corridor to the office. I knocked on the door again and again, a little louder each time, but still there was no answer.

"Dude, let me at it."

It was Dale, pushing through and before I could stop him he pushed the door with his shoulder while at the same time lifting the handle. He shoved at it and it gave just a little bit. He stepped back and kicked the door in. I took it that he was not a patient man.

I followed him in, expecting that an alarm would go off but nothing happened. I turned on the lights and pulled what was left of the door behind me. The reception area was cozy: a leather couch, coffee table with travel magazines, neatly fanned out at the top to look like a deck of cards. I walked over and started rummaging through the cabinets behind the receptionists' desk.

After going through several cabinets, I came across one marked "personnel.' I opened it. It had entries in it – names of people, men and women – possibly employees or clients that had been placed on various jobs, or perhaps it was a listing of job applicants. I thumbed through the names but nothing stood out. I turned over the page and scrolled down the list of names.

Dale, after a little while, stated casually that we needed to get the hell out of dodge, as he put it. We had overstayed our welcome. I needed a little more time but I knew he was right: we had done as much as we could. I just had to take the file.

I started walking to the door but Dale reminded me that we needed to wipe down our fingerprints. I retraced my steps and – using my shirt sleeve – begun cleaning whatever I had touched.

We were just about done when the decrepit door was pushed open and two men walked in.

"What do we have here?" one of them asked. He was black, his head shaven into a bumpy orbit. His partner, a mean – looking Mexican with a permanent sneer on his face, started slowly walking towards me. He was stocky but you could tell he did not have too much body fat.

"We should call the police," he said mockingly and then broke into laughter with his black friend joining in.

"Yeah, tell them we got ourselves here a break – in. Or we could just fuck them up, we don't want the man asking too many questions, eh?"

They looked at each other.

"That's not a bad idea. Perhaps we should call Bill?"

"No. Let's have some fun."

The black man pulled out what appeared to be brass knuckles. I did not think people still did that – it was the stuff made for relic B – movies. He made fists with them and as if on cue he lunged at Dale. The black man never saw what hit him. A right came crushing on his skull and I knew even before he hit the ground that he was out cold.

The Mexican literally made a run at me like a rugby player coming in for a low tackle. I sidestepped and threw my right knee across his face but missed him. I backed up, trying to create some space where I could set him up for a combination. He ducked my right cross and awkwardly landed a slapping left hook into my mid – section. The pain shot up my spine and before I doubled over in pain, he followed up with a wild right. He caught me on the way down and sent me sprawling into the receptionists' desk. I struggled to my feet and when I finally made it, I saw the Mexican coming towards me again.

"Hey, *muchacho!*" It was Dale calling out. The Mexican stopped, turned and saw Dale walking towards him with his arms to his side – casual.

The Mexican started to reach behind his back with his right hand. I knew that he was going for a gun. I took two quick steps towards him and landed a right to his jaw but that did not seem to faze him. He pulled out a gun – and as he started to point it at me, Dale was on him. With his big hands, he wrestled the gun and clocked him with the butt of it. The Mexican's legs gave way and Dale clocked him again for good measure, dropping him in a heap next to his friend.

"Let's go!" Dale whispered sharply.

I stood up and walked over to the black dude and went through all his pockets, looking for an ID and anything else that might help. He did not have much on him – a business card, some keys and a smartphone. I placed those in my pockets and walked over to the Mexican who was now rubbing the back of his head.

"You are both dead!" he said between breaths. "Do you hear me? You are both dead!" he repeated, his sneer interfering with his syllables.

"Just ask him where your sister is, man, we ain't got all day." Dale was standing by the door on the lookout.

"I'm not going to tell you shit, Amigo, *nada!*"

I knelt in front of him and asked him quietly if he knew where I could find Azani.

"I don't know anyone name Zane or whatever!"

"Where can I find her?"

He looked at me contemptuously and said, "I won't tell you shit!"

He then spat at my feet. I was about to slap the hell out of him when I caught Dale at the corner of my eye. Before I knew what he was doing he was standing next to the Mexican with a gun on his head.

"Where is the girl? You have up to three. One...!"

Five minutes later we were headed to a place the Mexican had called The Farm.

Chapter Eleven

After what seemed like a long drive, we pulled up in front of a huge gate and two armed guards approached the red Mustang. Dale gave them the password: "Little Birds." The Mexican had told us that that's all we needed to get in – a password that The Farm patrons paid for discreetly, with thousands of dollars in advance, but which we had extracted from him at gunpoint. I held my breath. Supposing he had set us up?

The guard stood back as if he was inspecting the car and then leaned into the driver's side.

"That is one sweet ride," he said and then waved for his buddy to lift the gate to let us through.

We pulled up to the entrance of what appeared to be a hotel. A valet, in complete uniform ran to the driver's side and opened the door. Dale jumped out and I followed from the passenger side.

"Welcome to The Farm, Sir," the valet said, handing Dale a ticket for the car as he took the keys.

"Thank you."

"How long will you be, sir?"

Dale flashed a smile before answering.

"Just a couple of hours, and if all is well, we might prolong our stay."

"Enjoy yourselves and once again, welcome."

Dale handed him a tip and we walked in through the front door where we were greeted by two topless young women who took our arms and walked us down a little corridor and into a reception area, complete with a bar where big screen

TVs mounted on all walls showed soft pornography, college football, old basketball games and NASCAR races.

"Table or counter?" one of the naked girls asked.

"Table, please," I answered.

As soon as we were seated, a waitress came to take our order. She was wearing shorts and sneakers but nothing on top. As she walked away, I noticed that her shorts were bare in the back. I turned to say something to Dale but was interrupted by a woman's voice.

"Hello there, sexy!"

I turned to see an Asian woman standing almost behind me. She was wearing a red see – through kimono. With almost everything laid bare for my eyes. I looked around and then back at her. Nice figure, interesting neckline – kissable but nothing to write home about – legs, long for her size and brown leather sandals that showed off two pointy toe nails – in black.

Her smile revealed a nice set of teeth, almost too good to be originals. She was not bad looking but she was wearing too much make – up and a very strong perfume. Well, well!

My mind was playing those angles when I was interrupted by the feedback from a microphone she was holding as she addressed the crowd.

"Hello? Hello...is this one...ah...okay...Gentlemen, welcome to the Farm. I am your hostess, Agnes. Whatever is your pleasure, please do not hesitate. You will find that we have almost anything you can ever want and we have taken all precautions to make sure that your stay here is not only enjoyable but also safe and discreet. You are in exclusive company, as you know from your sponsor."

There was a slow clap and then some laughter.

We did not respond, not knowing if the Mexican had omitted some details. She then gave the microphone to the bartender and turned her attention to us.

"Oh, I see, this must be your first time with us," she said, smiling knowingly. "Don't you worry, we take really good care of our guests and our girls know what to do."

The waitress brought our drinks. I sipped on my rum and coke. Dale had asked for a shot of tequila for starters, and a St. Arnold to chase it down. He licked a little salt off his left hand, threw the drink down his throat and quickly chewed on a lime to take the sting off the tequila. His big hands now looked gigantic holding an empty shot glass between his index finger and his thumb but he did not seem to mind at all.

"This way, gentlemen, please follow me." Agnes said with a casualness that was at once calming and enchanting.

She begun to walk and we followed, catching up to her. She held Dale by his waist and asked him what he preferred. And I figured out what she meant...

"I like them thick; you know, with some meat on them, something I can hold on to."

"What about you? You look like you could use a good lay."

She was looking dead straight at me.

I swallowed.

"I'd like a black girl, preferably international. I seem to relate better with someone like me – it's a black thing."

I gave her a forced smile and a nod.

"Whatever you like, sir. We are here to accommodate your wildest fantasies. Now, if you gentlemen will go into the lounge, I will send some girls out. You pick whichever girl or girls you want. There are private rooms in the back of the hallways over there and if you prefer group therapy, you can take your girls to The Burrow, over there," she said pointing to the right.

She was all business. And that scared me a little but she soon then left and we proceeded to the corridor leading to the lounge.

The doors to it opened automatically. I was the first one to walk in and I headed straight to the bar but I stopped short – it took me a minute to come to terms with what my eyes were feeding me. To my right, I caught a glimpse of a half – naked man groping at the thighs of a half – naked woman. Just next to them, a topless girl was giving two men a lap dance while on the other table, two girls were stroking the balding head of an Asian man while his friend was kissing their breasts.

"What the fuck is this?" Dale asked, his eyes darting all over the place.

I took a deep breath and said, "What do you think?"

"Holy shit, man, we are in the thick of it," Dale whispered back.

I looked over to the left and it was the same – men and women huddled together, touching and kissing young girls. Other patrons sat on love seats and couches that lined the outer walls watching porn flicks while their ladies massaged them suggestively before disappearing into the private rooms. Others did not make it to the rooms and went about their business right where they were!

I continued walking to the bar and sat down. To the right behind the bar was a stage, complete with a stripper pole on which several naked women danced – taking turns at the pole while men and women threw dollar bills at them.

Dale pulled out a bar stool and sat down next to me and we ordered more drinks.

"Gentlemen, meet your new friends."

It was Agnes, who was now accompanied by five girls wearing nothing but thongs. I swallowed, not knowing what to say or do. Dale turned and smiled – a smile that told me he had forgotten how and why we were here.

"Well, well, let me see," he said, rubbing his hands together.

He sized the girls up the same way one does produce at the supermarket. He pointed at a well – rounded Asian girl and, as an after thought also picked the white girl with big eyes. That left me with the other three – two black girls and a Spanish – looking little thing that looked to be underage and frightened, despite that forced smile on her plump face.

I sipped on my drink and said hello to them. They stared at me, their lips smiling and eyes that had no life in them. I felt sorry, angry and despondent. But I had work to do.

I asked the two black girls to stay. A smiling Agnes and the Spanish girl walked away. I downed my drink and asked for another one and as the waiter busied himself, I asked the taller of the two girls to a private room. As soon as my drink came, I picked up my drink and signaled to Dale to stay put. He had this goofy look on his face that told me that he was not going to.

The girl slipped her hand into my waist and guided me towards the back and we found an unoccupied room. There was a small night stand next to a queen – size bed with satin sheets and not much else. I placed my drink on the stand and pulled the little drawer expecting to find condoms. There was none: just a copy of the Bible.

I sat on the bed. She came and stood in front of me, placing my hands on her breasts. They were nice and firm but I managed to pull my hands away.

"What do you like sir? I will do whatever you..."

"Can we talk first?" I asked quietly.

My voice quivered but I did not give a damn – this was life and death and there was no easy way to establish a line of communication quickly and build trust so that I could get some information.

She looked disappointed, perhaps being used to men who came to her quickly and left just as fast.

"What do you want to talk about?" She managed to ask.

"Tell me about yourself."

"I like to dance, I like to give..."

"No, I mean like where are you from?"

"Where do you want me to be from?" she asked, perhaps thinking I was role – playing.

"Tell me, why do you do this?" I asked, hoping to put her on the defensive but I knew it sounded wrong the minute I finished asking it.

She looked at me for a few seconds, perhaps deciding how to handle this situation. I thought I detected a glint of surprise, perhaps more from the irony of the question.

"Why are you here?" she asked playfully.

She smiled – a thin smile that lit up her face but quickly disappeared. She then placed her fingers on my thigh and started rubbing back and forth, slowly and with each pass, they came closer and closer to my crotch. I tried to will myself to not feel the sensations but without much success. I pushed her hand away.

"Well, I like giving pleasure. You look like you could use a hand. Just relax and let me make you happy." She was smiling.

"I don't want to be happy." I blurted out.

That startled her.

I smiled and said, "What I mean is, not yet."

"Ok, you are the boss." She sounded disappointed but I detected relief – perhaps appreciating the fact that she could use a little break. "But just make sure that Agnes knows that I did what I could for you – whatever it is that you want – or don't want. I can get in trouble."

"She does not have to know, does she?"

"I'm just saying. No one messes with her."

"Don't worry, I got your back. Now you must do something for me… No, not that. Just hear me out and don't be alarmed. I am looking for a girl, a Kenyan girl who might have been brought here not too long ago."

She jerked her head back and sneered at me.

"Excuse me?" she said with her lips pulled down towards her chin.

"I am not here for this…I am here to get…just help me. Her name is …"

"Sh! No names, please don't tell me."

Her eyes shot out into round orbits, her eyebrows arched in fright. Only a person who has seen the repercussions of disclosing information could have been that scared but I had to press on.

"Can you help me, please? She is my sister!"

She sat up from the bed and looked at me. Her eyes shone in the dim lighting but her face had softened just a little from the initial reaction.

"You are crazy! You don't know Agnes...or these men. Please, you better leave, now!"

But she did not make to leave.

I knew I was getting to her – she was offering me advice on the dangers that lay ahead.

"Don't tell anyone but I need to find her before it is too late. Surely you would want someone to help your sister if they could, right?"

She thought about it and then said, "I don't want any part of this. Please leave me out."

She said it almost like a whisper – she was not completely refusing but she was not in agreement either – she needed some reassurance and some gentle nudging but before I could think of a good way to marry the two, she turned and started to walk out. I jumped up on my feet and stopped her at the door.

"Hey, please, just tell me how to find her." I whispered to her as soon as I caught up with her.

"I am not going to tell you anything – they will kill me."

She then turned back to face me, brought her face to my ear.

"There's a new girls initiation in the Burrow later on tonight, perhaps you will find a girl you like there."

She walked out.

Just as I had suspected, Dale was nowhere to be found. I sat down and contemplated my next move. I could not ask for Azani by her name or country without raising some suspicion. My only option was to take my chances in the burrow – but I needed to know where Dale was in case we had to get out of here in a hurry. I sent one of the girls to find him and a few minutes later, a smiling Dale came sauntering to where I was with his two girls.

"Man, is this great or what?" He smacked the white girl's behind playfully and laughed gratuitously. I wanted to remind him that we were here on a different mission but instead I reminded myself that he was doing me a favor and it was not a time for lessons on morality.

"Hey, Dale, keep your eyes open, man. Shit is about to go down."

"Don't worry, my man, I got you."

He started laughing again as we walked to the Burrow, and the sounds of techno – music which reminded me of my days at the Carnivore in Nairobi. We opened the doors to the full blast of music and as our eyes got used to the dim lighting it suddenly hit us.

What Agnes had described as 'group therapy" was an orgy. Everywhere you looked there was a couple, or a threesome or an odd group standing over a woman or some girl, watching, clawing, sharing, and cheering each other on with loud grunts. Others who preferred to go it alone played with themselves or with the help of a companion while others watched from the counter or just gazed at the big screen TVs showing hardcore porn. I had never seen anything like this. Even the sex parties we used to hear about when I was a student at the University of Nairobi could not have been anything close to this, I imagined.

We walked in and found an opening at the bar – it seemed to be the safest place. I sat down and Dale pulled the two girls close to him, one on either side lest someone decide to help themselves to one of them.

With all this madness going on, how the hell was I supposed to find Azani?

Before the waiter got to us to take our drink order, the loud music subsided and then some lights came on to my right and I turned to see what was happening. The lights illuminated a runway at the end of which was a small stage. The orgy seemed to come to a quiet stop, just a few grunts here and there, and slowly most of the naked and half – naked patrons walked and stood along the runway on both sides.

"What's happening?" I asked one of the girls.

"They are bringing in the new recruits."

"What do you really mean?"

"The new girls – this is how they introduce the new ones from all over and you can pick the one you want to take with you to your house or to your business, if you know what I mean. This is like a wholesale."

"They decide who goes and who stays and who gets sold for how much." The other girl added with casual indifference, "If you are lucky, you get to go away from the hell holes."

"Hell holes?"

The music grew louder and then the girls were paraded out one by one to the shouts, jeers, groping hands of men with lust and hate in their eyes. Some girls, their faces showing resigned fate did not even try to cover their nakedness with their hands but marched on stage holding a number in front of them and waited for whatever lay ahead for them. But many, with tears in their eyes tried to cover up their private parts with the palms of their hands but the men swiped their hands away the same way one swats at an irritant fly.

On the far end of the stage was a sitting area, almost like a VIP section where a group of men and women, white and black, clad in business suits and evening gowns sat quietly watching the parade. Behind them, I saw what I assumed were Middle Easterners wearing their long robes and turbans mixed in with your regular pimps – tight, shiny outfits, brim hats and wing – tip shoes. They were all busy scribbling some notes into writing pads as they watched the girls. I later learned that they were making silent bids – purchasing human beings for their harems or whorehouses.

I remembered the girl I had seen on TV back home – the one who had escaped from her bondage as a sex slave. This is the hell she must have gone through before being sold off to serve the fantasies of some bastard somewhere in Saudi Arabia.

I was about to make a move when I saw her. I recognized her even before she came to full view and into the groping hands. She was naked, her young tender breasts sticking out of her chest like small mangoes. Her face was hard and she looked straight ahead. She looked like a shadow of the happy – go – lucky girl we had seen leaving the offices of M International.

I had to act, and act fast.

"Dale, that's her."

He had a huge grin on his face until he looked up and saw her. His face changed and I saw him move his hands from the waist of the two girls. He then shifted from looking at Azani's nakedness, instead looking into vacant spaces between the groping hands and the balding heads in front of us bobbing in delight.

"Go get Agnes for me, please." I asked the girl to my right.

"Are you sure you want to mess with her?"

"It's okay. We are cool like that."

Agnes must be a key player, I thought to myself. The girls seemed to be either genuinely afraid of her or they hated her guts. I had to watch her closely.

I inched across towards the stage and when I was within earshot, I shouted a greeting in Kiswahili to Azani but she did not hear me at first and I shouted again over the music and the jeering. She looked my way but she did not make me out at first and then she saw me: our eyes held for a brief second and where I had hoped to see a glimmer of recognition or perhaps hope, I saw scorn and disdain and then she walked past me before disappearing into curtains behind the stage. I was not sure that she had recognized me – not with the trauma she was experiencing.

"What's the plan?" Dale asked after all the new girls had been paraded.

Before I could answer him, the music died and a white man wearing a long multi – colored jacket appeared on stage with a microphone.

"Ladies and gentlemen, pimps and pimpettes," he started when the noise had died down, "My name is William Burrows, welcome to the Farm."

And there he was!

He continued, "From the looks of it, everyone seems to have their hands full and I hope you are all having a wonderful time. Make sure you get your fill before you return to your wives and your families and for those of you who are taking some of our merchandize home, please turn in your bids and when you are called in, please pay the cashier promptly so we can move along smoothly. And remember, we like cash around here. We will then make arrangements for your purchase to join you when you leave."

After a loud applause, he continued.

"Now, remember what we do here is offer a service, no pun intended, in confidence and trust and we intend to keep it that way. For our safety and yours, please refer only trusted friends – and those who can afford to be in such exclusive company. The password for the next romp will be given out using the same channels so make sure we have your contact. Thank you and please try to behave yourselves!"

With that, he walked behind some curtains and disappeared.

The music started playing again and as if on cue, the activities continued for those who had actually taken a break. I walked out of the Burrow. My best bet was to focus on Azani for now.

Dale found me at the counter sipping on a glass of water. I was glad to see him alone, having ditched his companions. He did not look up to meet my gaze but instead sat noisily on a stool next to me and asked me again what our next move was.

I had nothing planned but this much I knew: I was not quitting – and I was not leaving without Azani.

"We'll play it by ear," I said, speaking more to myself than to Dale. "If I can get her isolated, then perhaps we can make a break for it."

"The way I see it, there is one of two ways out of here," Dale responded. "One is to walk out that door, get in my car and drive away into the plains. Or two: in body bags."

"We will make it out, don't worry." I said unconvincingly.

My heart was pounding and in my mind I knew the best thing for us was to walk out, drive away and get help – let the chips fall where they may. But how could I leave Azani here?

Dale looked around as if he was trying to assess our options.

"Do you want me to go in the car and get my piece?" He was looking me straight in the eye, looking for a signal that would push him one way or the other. He was dead serious. A decision had to be made.

"Let's just stay put, eyes open and ready to get the hell out of here."

"Out of dodge!"

"Who?"

"The saying – let's get the hell out of dodge."

I smiled at Dale. He was trying to lighten the tension but I was too nervous to appreciate it.

It seemed to me that time had slowed down at the exact time that I needed things to move. I sipped on my water again and as I put my glass down, someone put their arms around me and just as the heavy perfume hit me she said;

"So, you have not found anyone or anything that you fancy?"

"Oh! Hi, there Agnes." She had startled me. I swallowed hard and wiped some perspiration off my forehead. "No, no there is plenty here to keep me happy."

"So what is the problem?" she brushed my face with her lips. She must have doused herself in perfume.

"Just having some difficulties, you know?" I choked.

"Oh, you mean your boy will not come out to play?"

I did not protest – she had given me a possible way out.

"It happens."

She smiled knowingly, reached into her purse and pulled out some blue pills. She handed me one.

"Make sure you have someone with you in thirty minutes" she said with a laugh and started to walk away.

"Oh, yeah!" I stopped her. "There was the black girl who walked in with the last group of girls in the Burrow. Could you arrange that one for me?"

"What was her number?"

"What number?"

"The girl, she was holding her number, what was it?"

"Oh, yeah, number thirty three, I think."

She looked into a note pad she was holding, flipped through some pages and then checked something off.

"She might already be taken," she told me. "Are you sure you don't want to sample some other pussy? You know what they say about white girls, or even Asian…"

She sounded like she was talking about food or car parts but I did not let her finish.

"Black, baby, always bet on black," I insisted, using a line I had once heard in a movie.

"I'll see if she's still available. Are you sure you don't want to sample something different?"

"Perhaps next time," I said.

"Suit yourself but if you want, I can get you something new – you know the drill with new merchandising – if you break it, you must take it with you."

She took two steps and then stopped and turned around.

"You are new at this, aren't you? Perhaps your sponsor did not explain how things work here, did he?"

"He was loud and clear but I obviously did not expect the level of service and excellence that I've witnessed," I said as I threw the pill into my mouth to show her that I was ready to play ball.

I had not intended to throw it that far back but in my haste to prove that I belonged here, I missed my mark – it hit the back of my tongue and found its way down the hatch. I reached for a glass of water and washed it down, hoping that I would make the bathroom and force myself to throw up before it found its way into my system. The last thing I needed right now was a four – hour erection.

She walked away. But I knew she was going to be watching me or have someone do it for her. I stood up and walked to the bathroom. I found an empty stall, walked in and pulled the door behind me. I was about to put a finger in my mouth to induce vomiting when I heard a whimper from the stall next to mine. I hesitated and then I heard the growl of a man demanding some kind of service.

"Come on baby, do it and do it slow!" It was the guttural request of a man in the throes of desire.

"No, I am not going to… I don't do that!"

"What the fuck do you think you are? You are a whore, bitch! You do as I say or I will take you back to William and demand my money back. And then we will see how that goes for you. Now start, slowly."

"Yeah, tell Williams see if I care. I only work for him!"

I opened my door slowly and walked towards the commotion. The door was ajar so I pushed it open slowly and peered in. There was a naked, stubby white man standing on the toilet seat and in front of him stood a black girl whose head he was pulling towards him while she was pushing herself away from him, resisting. He was the first one to see me and he smiled at me with teeth that needed work.

"This is a feisty one but wait your turn if you want to have a go!" He said, barely getting the words out through his clenched teeth as he tried to push himself into the girls' mouth. She turned away, pushing him with her forearms and that's when I saw her face. It was Azani!

I quickly two – stepped and pulled her away from Stubby who, desirously dazed, had thought I was coming to his aid. So he did not expect it when I pivoted to my left and came up with a left hook to his jaw, knocking him clean off his throne. His head hit the back wall of the bathroom and he fell forward, collecting in a heap beneath our feet.

Azani was about to scream but I placed my hands on her lips. I had come to rescue her, I said reassuringly, and then asked her to follow me quietly.

"I will explain later, please just come with me."

"I don't know you. I can just leave."

"Listen, we have to go right now. We don't have much time…"

"Where are we going?" she asked, skeptically.

"My name is Jack Chidi. I am with the *Daily Grind* back home in Nairobi. Don't you remember me?"

"Who sent you and where are we going?" she asked again.

I had worked out a plan in my mind: we would sneak out, hop onto Dale's car and get the hell out.

"Me, like this?" she asked, almost bemusedly. "Naked girls do not simply walk out of The Farm and into the sunset," she added, a little more composed than earlier.

Oh yes, Azani was almost naked. She was right of course. There is no way she was walking out without calling attention to us.

I turned and motioned her to the clothes the naked stocky man had been wearing; they were neatly folded and placed on top of the cistern. Azani tried the black pants on first but they were short and came up to her shins – reminding me briefly of the King of Pop. She then put on his vest and his shirt before looping the tie around her neck. She seemed to be trembling but then again so was I! For both of us, it was from a mixture of relief and the odds ahead. She looked at herself in the mirror.

"I don't know if this will work," she whispered.

"It's the best we can do under the circumstances," I whispered back, conscious of the constraints.

I stepped out first and just as I was about to enter the lobby, I saw Agnes walking briskly to where I had been sitting with Dale. Behind her was a skinny black girl with a bad hair-do. She was wearing a red dress that clung to her like shrink – wrap on a canoe. Had she been standing behind a huge window at a clothing boutique, she would have done for a mannequin. I stopped short and Azani bumped into me but I was able to hold ground and I pushed her back into the bathroom.

"Just wait in here. Lock yourself in and be as quiet as a church mouse."

She looked at me, strangely – a cross between fright and confusion.

"You'll come back, right?" she asked.

I nodded reassuringly. Buoyed up by her confidence in me, I stepped out and walked towards Agnes who was all smiles.

"This one should do you just fine," she said laughing a little before lighting a cigarette and walking away.

I looked at the skinny black girl with the bad hair – do. She smiled at me and then sucked her index finger, as if trying to seduce me. Her face was small, like a small triangle. She had heavy make – up on, trying to cover up her acne. For such a small frame, she had long arms that she now threw in the air in mock frustration when I asked her to stop the finger sucking.

"What would you like then, big poppa?" she asked.

She pouted her lips, trying to look sexy, something she had obviously seen in those pornography videos they were showing all over the place.

"Just sit over there and be quiet for a minute while I talk to my friend here."

I walked over to Dale who was watching this spectacle with Skinny unfold.

"Hey, can you get the car and wait for me up front?" I whispered.

He did not wait to answer me.

"I'm way ahead of you but where is she at?" he asked.

"She's in the bathroom. Have the car ready to go, man!"

I looked at the skinny girl and asked her to join me. I slipped my hands into her skinny waist and as we walked to the bathrooms, she placed her hand on my crotch. That's when it hit me that the blue pill had kicked in and I was ready!.

"Oooo!" she said.

"Oh, just hush up!"

I was in panic mode. I had heard that the blue pill could send you to the emergency room and that the only way to stop such an incessant erection was to have blood drawn directly from the penis with a huge syringe.

As soon as we entered the bathroom, I heard a moan. It was Stocky coming to. I walked over to where he was and helped him up.

"What the fuck happened?" He asked, touching his sore jaw.

I did not have time to explain and neither did I want to. I pointed at the skinny girl and winked at him.

"But that's not who I paid for!"

"She's not going to fight you!"

He understood what I was saying to him. He smiled,

salivated and gave me a small salute. His hand was not the only thing saluting. As he stretched out his hands to Skinny, I decked him, a short right to his temple and he slowly crumbled to his knees before hitting his head on the toilet seat.

The girl let out a small shriek before covering her mouth with her skinny hands.

"What the hell are you doing?" she asked.

With her eyes now wide open, she looked like a red raccoon. I ignored her at first and then thought why the hell not.

"You want that on you?"

"It does not matter. Y'all the same to me and as long as I do what I'm told, me and my family will be ok. And I'll get paid."

If she wanted out, she had to come with me now, I offered.

"Do you know what happens to girls who run? Y'all must be crazy!" Skinny threw her arms up again before folding them in front of her small chest.

She looked genuinely scared. I had seen that same fear in the eyes of the girl on TV who had escaped what she called "hell" in Saudi Arabia. Well, here we were in the middle of it.

"Once we walk out of this bathroom, we head straight for the front door. Do not look around or like you are about to make a break for it – just walk normal, like you know what you are doing."

I was trying to sound in control of the situation but I was not fooling anyone. It did not matter to me – I was also in survival mode.

"I'm not going anywhere with you," Skinny declared, pouting her lips again.

"Listen, we have a small window of opportunity to get the

hell out of here. So it's your choice; come or stay."

I was getting a little irritated and I did not have the time to plead with her.

Just then, Azani came out. She was holding the oversized pants with her right hand to stop them from falling. She stood by the door, leaning against the stall – divider. I knew what she was going to say even before she said it.

"I think she is right. It is best if you go. It's too dangerous."

"Azani, I came all the way from Kenya and I am not leaving without you, period."

"Why?"

"It doesn't matter now, does it? I will explain once we get out. Let's go!"

"I can't go anywhere with you. It's too dangerous. I don't even know you. Besides you are in some serious trouble."

"Listen, I will explain everything. Right now I just need you to trust me."

I was getting very flustered. Somewhere, I had missed the trail of Mehta's killers, whoever they were, but I had stumbled onto something bigger: a major sex crime syndicate with roots in Kenya and the USA. Didn't she realize that she was its innocent victim? Couldn't she see that time was of the essence?

Just then I heard some movement. Stocky was coming to but I did not want to wait for him to regain consciousness to fight me and create commotion.

"Let's go!" I urged the two girls. Azani made to come then seemed to change her mind.

I made for the door but they stayed put. I jumped back in and took Azani by the hand – she seemed to need less cajoling.

"Are you in?" I asked Skinny.

She shook her head slowly.

I pulled Azani behind me and we walked out, leaving Skinny, arms crossed over her small chest, in the men's restroom, with Stocky slowly coming around.

In the lobby, I put my right hand around Azani's shoulders and pulled her tight next to me. She slipped her left hand around my waist and we headed for the front door.

We made it past the security guards and were just about to get to the door when I heard someone yell from inside.

"Hey, wait for me!"

I immediately recognized that voice even before I turned to see Skinny running towards us past the lobby, closely followed by a naked Stocky with arms outstretched, and gaining on her.

"Stop her! Stop her!" he shouted to the guards.

The guards moved from behind their desks and watched a white naked man chasing after a skinny little black girl in a tight red dress. One of the guards started laughing, placing one hand over his mouth and pointing at the white man with the other.

His partner, an over–weight bouncer, jumped into action and grabbed the girl just as she made it to the door. She kicked and squirmed in his arms and when the white man made it to where the guard was holding his prey, he realized that he was naked and all eyes were on him. Even the skinny girl stopped kicking for a while to look at the spectacle of Stocky in all his glory.

He quickly covered himself with his hands and stood there sheepishly, perhaps wondering whether to ask for the girl, who was now clinging to the bald black man for protection or turn back to the bathroom.

"He is well – endowed," a woman, who was watching said to a man standing next to her.

"I'll show you mine if you want," he answered.

She ignored him and continued gazing at Stocky.

Azani and I stepped outside. The commotion caused by Skinny and Stocky had diverted any attention from us momentarily. Dale had not pulled up yet and every second that passed felt like forever. Where was he?

I looked back towards the door. The security guard was dragging Skinny back to the lounge with Stocky following, his hands still covering his penis.

Just then I saw Agnes running towards the door followed by security personnel, guns drawn. I had not seen these guys before. It was then that I saw the security cameras – small black domes on the ceiling – they had been on us all along. I knew right away that the security guys were coming after us.

I let Azani's waist go. I did not know how to get out of this one. I decided to let it play itsself out. It was time to give up.

Then I heard the squeals of rubber on asphalt and turned around to see Dale pull up. I literally dragged Azani across the pavement, opened the back door of the car, shoved her in and then jumped in after her. Dale did not wait for the door to close. He floored it and we zoomed off, leaving a trail of smoke behind us.

I heard the unmistakable bursts of gunfire and the rear window shattered, spraying shards of glass inside the cabin. Azani screamed, grabbed me and we both crouched in the back seat.

After a short while I heard nothing but the roar of the engine. I lifted my head up to see what was happening behind us. The headlights behind looked like two dots in the distance. Just as Dale went through the front gates of

The Farm, the loud clanking of metal against metal sounded like an explosion. We hit a bump on the road. Azani and I were tossed up into the roof of the car and landed awkwardly on top of each other.

Dale jammed on the brakes as we came to the highway, turned sharply to the right, making the tail end of the Mustang spin. He then hit the gas and the tires squealed loudly into the night. Once we had traction, the Mustang tore into the highway picking up speed with every second.

Perhaps it was time to call the police and let them take over from here, I thought to myself but that would involve getting entangled in the legal system of a foreign country. And who knew just how well connected these guys were? How could they operate such a vast illegal enterprise and not draw attention from the authorities?

Dale interrupted my thoughts. He cursed loudly and then slammed the steering wheel with his right palm.

"What's wrong?" I asked, instinctively looking behind us. There was just darkness following us in the night.

"We need gas!"

"Oh shit, how much do you have?"

"She will carry us for another ten miles – we have to pull in at the next gas station coming up."

Just great, I thought to myself. We drove a little ways and Dale pulled into a BP gas station. He ran in and paid the cashier and as soon as the pump was ready, I started filling up. I pressed hard on the lever, trying to coax the petrol to pump faster but it was like watching grass grow. Dale ran back and jumped into the passenger side and opened the glove box. I knew he was searching for his piece. He checked the clip for bullets and then cocked. Then he pulled out the gun he had taken from the Mexican and handed it to me.

"I hope you know how to use it," he said.

I did not have time to raise my objections to guns. It felt odd and at the same time reassuring. Just point and shoot, Mburu had always told me, but I knew there was more to it than that.

"I think we should call the cops and report a homicide at The Farm," said Dale. "That way they have to respond, perhaps even send in SWAT."

"Wouldn't you have to ID yourself?" I asked doubtfully.

"Make the call, Jack," he ordered. "You can use the emergency call box inside. Just dial 9 – 1 – 1."

Yes, it was best that I reported this and kept Dale out of it. After all, Azani and I would be leaving the country in a matter of hours.

"Okay, here, get the gas while I make the call."

I knew I could not use my cell phone. There was no point in leaving a trail behind us. The fewer the identifiers, the better before this whole thing blew up. The last thing I needed was to be in some Texan Police station answering questions. And moreover, I suspected that this operation was too big not to be connected somehow with some people with enough pull to turn the tide against me.

I walked into the gas station and headed for call box. There was a huge concave mirror hanging in the corner directly behind the counter and as I walked in, I caught my contorted reflection in it – bowlegged and all. The clerk's reflection did not fare any better and had it been under different circumstances, I would have made a comment.

He was standing behind a thick wall of glass with a small opening for handling transactions – cash, cigarettes and an assortment of behind – the – counter merchandise including condoms and birth control pills. I noticed the security camera on top of the cigarette case.

The store was well stocked with all kinds of snacks, sandwiches, beer and canned goods for people on the go. The sight of a hotdog grilling station where beef franks rolled slowly, their fat content oozing onto the metal rollers and into a collection basket below, made me feel suddenly hungry.

The Asian clerk behind the counter eyed me closely.

"I just need to use the phone," I said as I walked past. I had seen his hand go under the counter and I knew that he was reaching for his piece.

Just then I heard loud bangs coming from outside and I jumped back, crashing into the hotdog stand. The clerk pulled out a shotgun and through the opening on the bulletproof glass he aimed it towards me, shouting some obscenities. I ducked down and yelled for him not to shoot, that the bad guys were chasing us when we ran out of gas. He did not hear any of that.

"Get out of my store, motherfucker," he shrieked excitedly. "You come here to rob me? I'm calling the police."

"Go on and call the police!" I shouted back. "That's what I was going to do. The bad guys are after us. I'm a journalist."

"No, you try to confuse and rob me. Not to tonight, nigger!"

It sounded funny coming from an Asian dude but I felt it nonetheless. I felt the "animal" stir. Who the hell was he calling nigger? I had to let him know that I was not going to be insulted but his gun was asking me to think of a different way to handle the situation.

Two more shots rang out from the outside and a bullet hit the front window of the store shattering it. I heard the clerk yell out some more some obscenities.

"Call the police!" I shouted.

He did not respond so I looked into the round concave mirror and saw him ducked down, holding the shotgun between his legs and the phone on the other. I crawled towards the door, opened it looked outside. Dale was hunkered down, on the driver's side that faced the store, leaning on his car, gun in hand. I saw headlights a little ways behind his car – two more shots hit Dale's car. He quickly stood up and returned fire before ducking down again.

I heard the clerk yelling on the phone, something about an attempted robbery and a shoot – out outside his store.

"Yes, it is a black man…he is still in the store…No, but I'm sure he had one…that he was a journalist and that they are being chased…please hurry, they're still shooting outside…"

I had to get out.

I called out to Dale to cover me. He counted down to three with his fingers. I braced myself and as soon as he stood up to give me cover, I half – stood and ran as fast as I could to where he was and flopped down beside him.

"Let's get the hell out of here!"

"No shit!"

He re – loaded his gun. And then I remembered Azani. Where the hell was she? Was she still in car? Was she hit? I looked around, trying to find a way to escape. We needed the car but we could not just get in and drive away. Our safest place had been inside the store but for the Asian clerk with a bad attitude and a shotgun.

I pulled out the Mexican's gun and held it with both hands. Point and shoot! I said to myself.

The store clerk came running through the door, with his gun, shoulder high and aimed at us. I heard the click – click of a shotgun loading. Dale turned around and when he saw the Asian, he started to point his pistol to take him out but before he could get aimed, the shotgun blast exploded. Boom! I ducked down instinctively, bracing for the shells and shrapnel. I rolled over and pointed my gun at the Asian, closed my eyes and pulled the trigger. Nothing.

The next thing I heard was Dale shouting at me to get up and run! I opened my eyes just as he grabbed my arm and helped me up. He pulled the passenger door open and jumped in and across to the driver's side. I followed him in and we took off, followed by a hail of bullets. As we zigzagged past the clerk, I saw him raise his shotgun one more time but before he could take aim I saw his body buckle, his knees giving way. He raised his gun again and this time I heard the gunshots and saw his body jerk before it hit the pavement as we sped off into the darkness.

"Next time you point your gun at someone, make sure your safety is off," Dale said, not even looking at me. I turned around and asked Azani if she was okay. She said she thought so and that was good enough for me.

Chapter Twelve

Irene opened the door and let us in. She had earlier pulled her car out of the garage so Dale could keep his out of sight at my request.

"You seem to invite trouble everywhere you go, young man!" She admonished me jokingly.

She then invited us to some tea. I asked her if she had something stronger. Frayed nerves need something to steel them. She poured me a shot of Glendale's whisky and offered Dale the same. Azani abstained, saying that she needed to clean up first. Irene invited her to use the guest bathroom and said that she would lend her some of her clothes to wear. They walked upstairs and after a few minutes Irene came down and joined us.

"You've had quite a day, I see," she looked over at Dale.

He was holding his drink between his legs, his feet crossed at the ankles.

"Yeah, it was quite something, right here in the good old US of A," he responded, downing his drink and wiping his lips with the back of his hand.

There was a lull in conversation so I stood up.

"I have to call Bulldog and Detective Dube," I said. "We are going to need some serious help."

"Yeah, we are in some really deep shit!" Dale said and then asked Irene if he could have another drink.

"Yes, please, don't ask," Irene said. "And let me get you boys some towels so you can clean up."

She got up and walked to the bedroom. I followed her. I would make my phone calls after I had thought everything through.

"Irene, please forgive me for bringing…"

She did not let me finish.

"I am just glad you are okay," she cut in.

She turned around and gave me a hug. It felt good – it was the best I had felt all day. I tried to thank her but my mouth went dry.

I put my hand on her lower back and pulled her to me. She pushed herself away and looked at me.

"You need a shower!"

"I know. Can I?"

"I'll get you a change of clothes from your bag."

I took a nice hot shower and after we were all cleaned up, we sat down for dinner. Irene had whipped up some spinach and cheese ravioli with sautéed chicken in a thick lemon – thyme sauce. It was the best meal I had had in a long time.

Irene was great company and all evening I kept my eyes on her. There was something about her that I found quite endearing. I remembered she had it the first time I saw her in Kikuyu – understated warmth and beauty.

"So, what the hell happened out there today, Jack?" Irene asked.

We were now sitting down in her living room. Azani was holding on to a cup of tea with both hands. She was wearing a dress Irene had given her. I could tell that she was uncomfortable and I tried to assure her that hers was a story that would end well – she had gotten out in the nick of time. I turned to Irene, feeling good about having rescued Azani but knowing that we were not yet out of the woods.

"Well, I am sure Azani will agree with me when I say we were in hell."

I did not wait for her to agree.

"I'm telling you this is bigger than we ever imagined. These guys are ruthless. Do you know that they killed your friend?' I said, turning to Azani.

"What friend?" Azani asked, startled.

"Lidia!" I said and then suddenly felt stupid, unfeeling almost.

Azani looked at me briefly and started sobbing, quietly at first then broke down.

"You said Lidia is dead? Who killed her?"

"The bad guys…you see, this is all connected to…"

"Who are they? Who killed her?" she asked again.

"I was hoping you could shed some light on this whole operation – at least on this end. You may be in danger from the same bad guys!"

"I don't get it. Why would anyone kill her? All she wanted was a job to help her family." Azani said, sobbing some more.

"It's not your fault, Azani; they tricked you, like they have tricked many of the other girls."

"I know, but I feel terrible about Lidia. It was not supposed to be like this," she wiped the corner of her eyes with a napkin.

Irene went to her and hugged her, trying to get her to calm down.

"How was it supposed to be?" Irene asked.

"They promised housing, good pay and adventure," she said then stopped and looked at me."It can be rough but the pay is good for the girls."

Was she trying to convince herself? I poured myself another drink and Dale asked for one as well. I did not want to rush the poor thing – the best thing was to wait for her to tell her story, but she obviously needed a nudge from me.

"You can tell us everything you know, Azani. You are among friends."

"They work with you?" she asked.

"No, no just friends, good friends, but without them I would not have been able to rescue you."

"Thank you all. I am very grateful. They said that they would help us with our passports and immunizations if we wanted an overseas assignment. That is where the good money was. Some girls stayed local but some wanted to see the world."

I had heard all that before.

"Did they pay you any money upfront?" I asked.

"Only to those girls whose parents were hesitant – they called it a loan program. They cover all our housing and food expenses and once a girl starts work they would handle their finances until one was ready to come home. They said one did not have to have money in one's pocket since they provided everyone with everything."

"How about threats or any use of force…" Dale jumped in.

"No, at first, they are very nice. But once you signed a contract, they said that they owned your time for the duration and that if you did not work or obey your employers, they would come after you or your family to get their money back."

She walked us through the hiring process, the mock interviews and testimonials given by girls who had since returned from their work abroad. They even brought some girls into the office to talk about their experiences.

"What about the pharmacy? You went there with your friend. What were you doing there?" I asked, hoping that her answer would shed some light on Mehta's involvement.

"We went there to get our shots, our passports and all other travel documents and some pocket money if we needed to give something to our families before we left."

She paused, sipped on her tea and then turned to me again.

"So, how is it that you come into this mess?" she asked, adding: "Risking your life even? What's in it for you?"

I sat up, finished my drink and told them about the call from Mrs. Mehta and how my investigation had led me all the way to Texas. After I was finished, everyone looked at me, and for a moment I drank in their admiration. I felt my heart leap up when Azani stood up and embraced me.

"I still don't know why you are so concerned about this, but thank you. How can I ever repay you for this? I hope we will meet up in Kenya!"

It was a bit awkward, what with Irene looking on but I allowed myself the moment.

"And you guys have been so helpful," she said turning to Dale and Irene. "I wish there was something I can do for you here in Texas... but God is great and I pray your good deeds will be rewarded, if not here then up in heaven."

It was quite moving and I was glad that we had extracted her from the bowels of hell.

We talked some more, trying to get to the bottom of it and what our best options were. Irene suggested calling the Kenyan Embassy in the morning to make arrangements for Azani to travel back home. Dale did not care too much about going to the authorities but I knew it was only a matter of time before they caught up to us – and then what?

Azani was the first to voice her exhaustion. Indeed she looked like she could use a good night's sleep, what with all she had gone through.

"I hope they don't come for me here!" she said.

Dale and I assured her that she had nothing to worry about – they would have to go through us.

"I hope it does not come to that," Dale said.

Irene walked her to the guest bedroom where I had slept the previous night.

I poured myself another drink and sat down next to Dale. He had his eyes closed. He deserved the glory. I was right in telling Azani that without him I would not have been able to rescue her.

I nudged him in the ribs.

"I bet you this is not what you had in mind when you volunteered to show me the sights and sounds of Texas, but I really appreciate you, man."

"Don't sweat it, man. I'm just glad I could be of some help. That's some fucked up shit, man. This is not what I fought for over there."

He paused and threw back his drink before continuing.

"I mean, one never really thinks how these girls end up working in strip clubs, or a street corner whoring for some pimp downtown. This is some sick shit, man. I'm glad we were able to get her out. And she appreciates our help. That's good enough for me."

He looked past me at a painting hanging on the wall behind me. It was an African woman holding a gourd tightly to her midsection. The gourd had small roots shooting from it that seemed to cement the woman to the ground she was walking on and then turned up and touched her face.

"What happens to the others, Jack? What happens to them now?"

I did not have an answer for him – there was no knowing.

Just then, Irene came and I asked her how Azani was.

"She's a lot stronger than she looks. She will be fine. But that bit about heaven was a little too much for me."

"Are you an atheist?"

"Not really, but I don't like going overboard with my beliefs." She said and sat down.

"May I use your laptop?" I requested. "I need to email Bulldog. I might not be any nearer solving Mehta's murder but this will definitely intrigue him enough – which might help if there are glitches with travel papers for Azani – he has connections."

"You don't have to explain. I keep the laptop in my bedroom – the password is my last name."

That was all I needed to get me out of there. In the bedroom, I sat in front of the computer, trying to piece the whole thing together – connecting all the dots, from Mehta, Mohali, Logic Placements, and The Farm. But how did all these relate to murder? Perhaps Mehta had found out the truth behind Logic Placements and had wanted out. That was enough reason for someone to want him dead. We now had a possible motive, who exactly had the opportunity besides Mrs. Mehta?

I was still brooding over the case when Irene walked in. She closed the door behind her gently and informed me that Dale had fallen asleep on the couch. I could tell she was getting tired as well so I excused myself and made to walk out.

"You don't have to go, just ignore me and continue doing what you were doing."

She walked into the master bathroom and after a short while I heard the toilet flush followed by the sound of running water and then incessant sound of an electric toothbrush. My mind started to paint a picture of her, imagining her in the bathroom taking a shower but I quickly forced myself away from such thoughts without much success.

I was getting too tired myself but I decided to wait for her to come out so I could thank her for all that she had done for us. I logged on to her laptop and checked my emails – nothing but the usual spam. I opened the online *Daily Grind* and skimmed the headlines but nothing caught my interest and so I logged off, leaned back on the chair and closed my eyes. I must have drifted away and dozed off.

"You look so peaceful with your eyes closed. What are you thinking about?"

She was standing in front of me. I had not heard her come in and she startled me.

"Wow, you clean up well," I smiled, sniffing the air around her.

She was wearing a black and red night dress. It flowed and then settled in around her, hugging her curves gently. I sat up and she gently placed her hands on my shoulder.

"You don't have to get up."

"It's okay. I was waiting to thank you."

"And how did you want to thank me?" she asked smiling.

I swallowed. Was she flirting with me?

I stood up to hold her but instead I felt myself poke her. I looked down and that is when I remembered the blue pill – it was in full effect and even the images of a huge syringe drawing blood could not bring me down. I held her hands in mine and re – positioned myself.

"Well, I figured by saying 'thank you' and also..."

"Oh my god, I can feel that." she whispered.

Her eyes were dancing in the light as she looked at me, softly, waiting for me to finish. I had no words left in me – I kissed her lips, gently – a touch really. I pulled back a little and noticed that she had closed her eyes and as she lifted her hands to my shoulders, I leaned into her and kissed her again – a little fuller this time and I felt her lips respond to mine. We slipped under the covers.

It was a while before we slept.

Chapter Thirteen

I was woken up by loud knocking on the door. I could not see well in the dimly lit room and for a few seconds I could not remember where I was but when she brushed my back with her fingernails, the wonder of the night came back. It felt good. I turned to give her a kiss but the knocking became louder and insistent.

"Hey!" I shouted, instinctively looking around for anything that could be used as a weapon. "Who is it?"

"Jack! Jack! Wake up, man. I think Azani is gone!"

It was Dale.

I jumped up and ran to the door and just as I was about to open it, Irene turned on the light and I realized that I was stark naked.

"Oh, you look cute!" she teased sleepily as I ran back, fumbling for my pants.

"I'll be right back, don't you go anywhere."

I gave her a quick kiss and walked out to find Dale in the hallway.

"What do you mean she is gone?"

He handed me a piece of paper and I read the note. It was addressed to me.

"Jack, thank you but please don't come looking for me. This is something I have to do for myself and my family. I will meet you back home someday. Azani."

Not again! I felt deflated, the note notwithstanding. After all we had done, we were back to square one – and to top it off, we now had some very angry people looking for us and the police surely trying to piece it all together.

"What is wrong with her?" I fumed.

"Jack, take it easy," Irene said as she walked in wearing a night gown. "It's called the Stockholm Syndrome."

"What the hell is that?" Dale asked.

"It's where victims identify and in fact sympathize with their attacker," Irene explained quickly.

We had come too far to get screwed by some irrational attachments to buggers like William and Agnes.

"Let me get some coffee going," offered Irene. "Why don't you boys turn on the TV and see if there is any news? By now the media will have picked up on last night's events."

We sat down, Dale and I, flipping through channels. My mind was racing. If she dared go back to the farm...I could not finish that thought. Lidia had done the same thing and we had lost her.

"How soon can you get your boys?" I asked Dale, remembering that he had offered such help earlier yesterday. He pulled out his phone and called.

Over a hurried breakfast, we played out different scenarios but only one thing seemed to make logical sense: we had to get Azani back!

I called Dube and after I relayed the events thus far, he reluctantly agreed to call the Kenyan Embassy and arrange for our extraction. It was time to get all systems ready – we were only going to have one shot at this and it was a long shot in the dark. I felt like a lamb returning to a lion's den and hoping for familial understanding.

"Irene, I don't know how safe this place will be, especially if Azani has talked to them. Perhaps you should consider..."

"I am not leaving," she answered stubbornly, cutting me short. "This is my home."

"Well, can you at least go somewhere safe for a while until things cool off?" I implored.

"It's okay, Chidi," she insisted. "I can take care of myself. You worry about yourself and your posse. Texas is big country and I know my way around."

Dale's friends arrived almost inside the hour. It was as if they had been on standby, waiting for that one call. I did not mind numbers on my side – and especially some mean – looking Texans with guns and itching for action.

I had expected an all – white crew but two of them, Terry and Gus were African Americans, and as Dale would explain later, they were all high school classmates, grew up in the same 'hood' and despite the racial tensions that flared up in Texas every once in a while, they had all managed to stick together – a band of brothers. Terry had also joined the Marine Corps and had seen action in Iraq before an IED had sent him home.

As Dale introduced us, I watched them closely, more from habit than anything else. I noticed that the one guy they called Bubba was looking at Irene with eyes that told me I needed to keep mine on him. He was not as big as Gus or Terry but he had a good size on him.

"So they call you JC down there in Africa?" he asked without a smile and with a very deep drawl that sounded like he was straining to let some gas out.

"No, they just call me Jack – or Chidi."

He thought about it for a second and then nodded his head. "I like that," he said without specifying which part he liked.

"This here is your little lady?" he asked, with his eyes still on Irene.

"Yeah, you could say that," I answered.

"I respect that. Man, she fine as hell!"

He gave her a huge smile and then winked at me, saying, "You devil, you!" He laughed and then turned to Dale and asked: "So what's popping?"

Dale asked me to explain. I did without giving up too much. They waited until I was done and then Gus asked me what I wanted them to do exactly. I paused, looking for a nice way of saying that I did not know but we were going into very dangerous territory.

"We understand that, JC, I mean Chi... what's your name again? Hell, my African brother – I ain't worried about all that. I just want to know what you want us to do."

Before I could answer Dale interjected.

"Let's just roll. Keep your eyes open and don't do anything unless you absolutely have to. Or better yet, follow my lead."

We decided not to take Dale's car – with the shattered back window, it would draw unnecessary attention. So we loaded into Terry's Ford Truck and headed towards The Farm.

"What's the plan, boys? 'Cause I'm ready as hell!"

It was Gus again and he reached under his seat and pulled out a tool box which he opened to reveal a small arsenal of weapons. He carefully inspected each and passed them out casually.

I was expecting heavy police activity along the route, especially at the gas station where the Indian attendant had been gunned down last night. But to my surprise we found the gas station was closed – with nothing there to indicate that any crime had been committed at all – let alone a murder. It looked completely deserted.

"Are you sure you guys saw any shit here?" Bubba asked.

"I know the fucking cops can cover up some shit but damn, it's like nothing happened here."

We drove on in silence except for Terry's humming of some gospel tune that I hardly recognized.

We came to the gate of The Farm and just drove in. The armed security guards that had stopped us the night before for a password were not there – which was odd. Perhaps we were being set up but we drove on, slowly, everyone looking out for any signs of trouble – guns ready.

We finally made it to entrance without any incident. A uniformed valet came to meet us.

"Welcome to The Mandarin," he said, giving us that smile that comes as a requirement.

I looked around me. Everything was different – from the uniform of the valets to the usher – an old Chinese dude wearing a long brim hat. There was nothing that hinted of last night. This was more family oriented establishment and I began to wonder if we had missed a turn and gone to a different resort.

"Excuse me, we won't be here long. I am here to meet with Mr. Burrows, William Burrows. He is expecting me."

The valet looked at me, puzzled.

"There is no Mr. Burrows here, sir," he responded, with that Texas drawl.

"I was with him last night."

"You were here for the Convention?"

"Yes!" I answered quickly.

He smiled and shook his head.

"Humph. How about Agnes, is she here?"

"Well, I don't know her either, but I don't work on Convention nights. They use a different company for valets and even inside help, so I don't know that I can help you.

Perhaps you may want to go inside and ask for Mr. Phillips, he would know."

I was not sure whether I should go in. What if this was a trap? Well, we were right in it so we might as well see it through – something fishy was going on here and we were going to get to the bottom of it, where I hoped, we would find Azani.

I turned to Gus, Terry and Bubba. They were now busy rapping along with a song playing on the stereo. Dale asked them to turn it off.

"You guys just wait here. If we are gone too long, you know what to do!"

I was not sure what he meant by that but it really did not matter now – we were way in too deep and the only logical conclusion was to follow through and see where we ended up.

The building looked pretty much like it did the night before, except that there were no naked men and women, boys and girls engaged in wild sexual acts and there were no girls being auctioned off to the highest bidder. Had we not been here ourselves just hours before, we would never have believed any tales of the sex trade.

"Wow, these fuckers clean up good!" Dale said as we walked through the lobby.

I was wondering about the same thing: how did they manage to vacate the premises, leaving not the slightest trace of their illegal activities? Something was very wrong with this picture. Even Houdini could not have pulled this one off without some major protection from higher up. Corruption was not just a Kenyan thing after all.

We were about to walk into the lounge area when from the corner of my eye I saw some familiar figure. I slowed down and pretended to watch something on TV. I then lowered my eyes and I saw the Mexican hunched over talking with a tall – looking white man – William Burrows. I quickly turned and headed in the opposite direction towards the bathrooms where I had rescued Azani just hours ago.

"You seriously don't think she is in the bathroom again, do you?" It was Dale, laughing.

"No, man, just follow me," I said quickly.

Dale looked behind us one more time before running to catch up me. After we had walked a little ways, I told Dale the Mexican was at the bar talking to William. We walked past the bathrooms, found an exit and quickly walked to the truck and jumped in.

"Anything?" Gus wanted to know.

"Oh we hit the mother – load!"

"You found her?" Terry asked.

"No, but we are onto something," I said.

I asked Terry to drive round the bend and come in again towards the lobby and park about a hundred yards from the entrance. From there we could see who was coming in or going out without being detected. There was no way we could miss the big Mexican, at least.

*****

I don't know how long we waited but as soon as the Mexican walked out, he lit a cigarette and paced up and down as he waited for the valet to get his car. He was joined by William who, after he finished talking on the phone, reached inside his pocket and handed the Mexican what appeared to be an envelope before he walked back in. Soon the valet brought a late model Toyota Prius and the big Mexican jumped in and drove off. We followed at a distance.

He drove quite fast but Terry was able to keep up with him and after about twenty five minutes on the Interstate Highway, the Mexican exited and took a service road for a few miles before turning onto Broadway Avenue.

He made a right onto a narrow street, slowed down and pulled up in front of a house with a well – manicured front lawn. He opened the garage, drove in and we watched as the garage door swallowed the little Prius. Perhaps this was his residence but it did not matter. We just wanted his cooperation.

After a few minutes or so a police patrol car pulled up to the house and an officer stepped outside and knocked on the door. The Mexican opened the door, stepped out and pulled it shut behind him. They spoke for a few minutes and then the Mexican reached into his pocket and pulled out the envelope he had received from William and handed it to the officer. He opened it, perused through the contents, shook hands with the Mexican and then walked back to his patrol car and drove off.

"I'll be damned!" Gus was shaking his head.

It was time to go talk with the Mexican. We pulled up next to his driveway and Terry parked the truck by the entry, blocking the narrow driveway just in case someone from the house decided to drive off. It also meant we could get to the truck fast if we needed to leave in a hurry.

Dale and I walked up the driveway and onto the front porch and knocked on the door. The Mexican instantly opened the door – perhaps thinking the officer had come back for something. He immediately recognized us.

"Aye Caramba!"

He jumped back and started to close the door but I stepped on the kick plate and pushed myself in. Dale was right behind me. The Mexican's eyes darted to a drawer next to him as he backed up away from us.

"I dare you to go for it," Dale said, calmly.

"Oh, no, homie, it's nothing."

"Who else is here?" I asked, looking around the living room. It was well kept, almost too neat. "Someone else lives here, I know," I added matter – of – factly.

"No, no, it's just me," he protested quickly.

Dale pulled out his snub – nosed revolver.

"You would not be lying to us, would you?" Dale asked, poking him in the stomach with the barrel of the gun.

"What do you want with me? You are going to get us all killed."

"No, you are going to get yourself killed unless you start talking."

As if to punctuate the point, Dale hit him once across the face with the butt of the gun. I did not think it was necessary and I was beginning to think Dale had something against the Mexican, but it did the trick.

"Ok, Ok! There are some girls," he said, adding: "I am a dead man. You guys don't know these people."

"No, we don't. Where are they holding the Kenyan girl?"

"Which girl? There are many girls and I don't know…"

"Where are the girls?" Dale asked.

The Mexican pointed to a door. I asked him to open it and we walked behind him down some steps leading to a basement. At the bottom, the Mexican hit a switch and that's when we saw them – girls as young as thirteen chained against the wall. From my initial count, I had them at twenty on each side of the room. I had not finished my count when I heard a toilet flush and a door opened up.

A nurse, complete with white uniform, stepped out.

"Oh, I did not expect to see you down here," she said grumpily, adjusting the innerwear under her frock. "There is no scheduled pick up until tomorrow. I wish you would tell me these things ahead of time."

She was an elderly Asian woman, perhaps in her sixties, with a thick Indian accent. She proceeded to go to a work station where she sat down lazily and started playing a game of solitaire with a deck of cards.

"Are these all the girls?" I asked her.

She looked at me and then at the Mexican.

"What is this, some kind of joke? Most of them left yesterday. These are the leftovers. You guys make my job hard, I tell you, very hard."

She wagged a crooked finger at me and then continued to play her game.

I looked at the scared faces of the children chained to the walls like dangerous animals. Some were lying on thin mattresses while others huddled together – the braver and oft times older ones, consoling the youngest amongst them who sobbed quietly or just stared into space. There were medium sized pail – buckets almost every three feet and in the middle of the room where girls from each side relieved themselves. This was the hell hole.

I felt the animal in me stirring. I thought about Azani, Mehta, the skinny girl from last night and next thing I knew, I was standing over the Mexican, watching him slowly crumble to the ground. I saw myself jump on him and begin to stomp on his face with my boots. I saw blood splatter on the cement floor.

"Jack! Jack! Get a hold of yourself!"

Dale pulled me off him.

"Unchain the girls," I ordered the nurse.

She quickly fumbled for some keys and begun unlocking the padlocks.

I walked up to the Mexican and knelt next to him.

As calmly as I could, I said, "I want names. And I want William!"

The Mexican had enough. He took us upstairs to his room and handed us a thumb drive. It turned out that he had kept a rudimentary log book as an insurance policy.

I made several copies and gave one to Dale – keeping the original and the others to distribute to News Agencies and law enforcement – the whole force could not be compromised – just a few bad apples.

The only way to blow this thing up was to have every agency we could think of getting involved. I called Irene and asked her to use all her contacts to get the news media here as quickly as possible. I gave her the address.

Using a phone book, I called the Texas Police Department and the local FBI field office while Dale called the Houston University Hospital and advised them to send several ambulances. I then called Immigration and Customs Enforcement at Irene's suggestion.

Next, we set off the fire alarm. I wanted the neighbors out here as witnesses in case somehow William sent in a posse crew to clean up – they seemed to be very good at it.

The girls, some of who had needed help walking outside, sat in the front lawn and waited. About three of them tried to make a break for it and it took some reassuring before they agreed to stay.

The Mexican had done enough but we wanted him as a witness and since we could not take him with us, I asked the Asian nurse to chain him up until the authorities arrived.

"What happens to me now? No job – nothing," she moaned.

"You can cop a plea or you can go to jail," I told her.

I did not feel sorry for her.

We left just as soon as we heard the sirens. There was no need for us to linger – we had done what we could for now and by the time the police sorted out this mess, I needed to be as far away as possible. I still had to get my case solved – even without Azani and as much as it pained me to leave without her, I had to get the hell out of Texas and out of the USA.

We picked up some Chinese takeaways on the way back to Irene's. The guys stayed with us late into the night. We tried to relay to Irene what we had seen but it seemed no words could capture the image, the stench, and the pain.

I pulled Dale aside and thanked him for everything he had done for me. I apologized for his Mustang but he said Terry and Gus would have it back to its former glory in a few weeks. They were excellent mechanics and Bubba's father owned a shop in a small town called Waxahachie where they would be going to lay low. I pulled out my wallet and handed him some large bills – it was not much but it would get him going. We agreed to stay in touch. Perhaps someday he could come visit me.

"Y'all crazy as hell," he said and laughed. "I like it!"

The next morning the busted sex trade ring was all over the news. The FBI with help from local authorities had raided six more safe houses where they found almost three hundred young men and women held in bondage.

I sat back on a sofa at Irene's and took stock of my situation. I had to leave Texas before the police or the media probe smoked me out. It would be hard leaving Irene behind and I said as much to her. But perhaps to make easy on me, she assured me that she would come visit in a few months. She still had her brother's place in Kenya and she said she needed to decide what to do with the property.

"If you live there, I can come visit often," I said.

"I don't know if I can keep up with you, young man," she said, smiling.

"Well, what can I say?" I said, smiling wryly, remembering the blue pill.

But I was not in a mood for light talk. I was thinking of my failure. I had not managed to rescue Azani; my attempts might even have sent her to her death, I thought, remembering Lidia's gruesome demise.

Under normal circumstances, I should have felt satisfied, elated even, with my cleanup job in Texas. But though arrests were made, there were two faces I didn't see among them: William and Agnes. They were still at large, probably being sought by all security agencies but that was not helpful to me at this time: I needed them in a place where I could ask them some questions. In reality, I was as far from solving the Mehta murder case as I was when I came here.

But the trip had more than confirmed that the sex – trade had probably cost Mehta his life. His murder had a Kenya – Texas connection. I had lost the trail in Texas but I knew that I could pick up the scent again back home in Kenya. I had to go back to Mohali: he was Mehta's silent partner, the man whose office had recruited Lidia and Azani. The man who, in all certainty, had ordered the arson that silenced Lidia.

I took the next flight out.

Chapter Fourteen

All roads lead to Mohali, I told Otieno and Jacob at the airport when I finally made it back two days later. Azani would meet Lidia's or Mehta's fate unless we acted fast, that is, if she was still alive in Texas.

Otieno sensed my anxiety and fatigue and restrained his curiosity about Irene. With just a question on how she was doing. We drove to the city where we had a hurried breakfast – scrambled eggs and sausage at The Fish Shack off Luthuli Avenue.

Otieno updated me on Mohali. His company, M International was registered with the Business Bureau as a Temporary Placement Agency whose sole responsibility was to place job seekers with employers for short term and long term assignments. The only difference between his and other agencies was that he was able to source overseas accounts.

"Murder International," I muttered but Otieno ignored me.

"He is an arrogant prick and one who seems to get what he wants when he wants it," he added, quickly furnishing details about Mohali's hectic schedule of meetings, lunches with different women and occasional dinner with his wife.

"Well, it's all about to blow up now!" I said.

I called Detective Dube and told him I was back in town.

"We need to meet up for a debriefing – I am sure you have more to tell me," he spoke presumptuously.

He did not sound too enthused but I figured he was being optimistically cautious.

"Sure!" I responded. "I hope you have something for me, too."

But I was not about to wait for Dube and his "something" before I acted on Mohali. So after I finished with Dube, I called Mohali's office and asked to speak to him.

"May I tell him who is calling?" a female voice asked.

"Yes, you may. My name is Jack Chidi with the ..."

"Oh, it's you again!"

"Yes, it's me again," I answered. "But listen very carefully. I am running a story on your boss."

"What story?"

"Tell him that it has a Texas connection," I replied provocatively. "And he can read it in tomorrow's paper. Have a good day!"

"Hey! Hold on! Don't you want to speak to him? Let me see if he's in."

I waited a few minutes and then she came back on the line.

"He would like to speak to you. You can come to the office, immediately."

I was not about to walk into his lair. We had to meet in a public place and I could not think of any better place than the New London Grill.

"Tell him I'll be waiting for him at the Grill in say, half an hour or so."

"I'll let him know."

Otieno and I stopped by the office. Bulldog was not in – which was a relief. Last thing I needed was explaining some shit I did not quite have a handle on. I checked my emails and then left for the London Grill.

I asked Ben for a booth just off to the side of the bar – a little privacy but where you still had a full view of the place.

"You know she is not working today, right?" he asked, referring to Meredith.

"Yeah, yeah," I lied, but was somehow relieved – I had secretly hoped not to find her there. But I knew we had to have a talk at some point.

After almost half an hour, a tall man walked in – alone. I watched him walk to the counter and talk to a waiter. After a few minutes, Ben appeared and after a few words he pointed the man in my direction. I recognized him immediately from Mehta's arraignment – the one who was paired with the Indian Man – Child.

He took off the sports jacket, folded it neatly on the back of the seat and sat down. Age had done a number on him but not in a bad way – just the usual wear and tear of living hard and fast. But underneath all that he looked like he visited the gym though not enough to be a prize – fighter.

"So… you are *the* Jack Chidi, eh?"

"That would be me…and you must be Mohali."

He smiled a little in acknowledgement.

A waiter came over to bring some menus but I waived him away.

"We can't even break bread together, Jack?" Mohali asked, letting out a small high pitched laugh that caught me off guard.

"You are not an easy man to get to," I started, "but let me cut to the chase; I know all about you and your so – called job placements. I have just come back from Texas – let's just say that William Burrows and I have met."

"You called me out here to tell me that?" he asked impatiently.

"I thought you asked to speak to me," I retorted. "Well, the way I see it, I think I have enough on you to have you put away for a while…"

He laughed – that high pitched laughter again.

"I hope you will still think it funny when the story is out and you are charged with murder!"

That caught his attention.

"Murder?"

"Yes, murder!" The word came easily.

He squirmed but played it off with a cough. He then looked around us before asking, "Why would I be charged with murder, Mr. Jack Chidi?"

"Vishal Mehta!"

He fidgeted again but this time he placed his hands on the table and clasped them together. They were huge hands with veins crisscrossing the back almost carelessly.

"Listen to me you…!" He caught himself. "I'm sorry. You have no idea what you are talking about." He swallowed loudly. "I am a businessman, not a murderer."

"We both know what's up," I said between clenched teeth.

"I don't know what you are talking about. I did not kill anyone!"

"Perhaps you didn't, but you ordered the hit. Either way you are going down for murder, prostitution, human trafficking, and racketeering…"

He raised his hands, interrupting me.

"I will not sit here and let you drag me into some bullshit!"

But he did not move, so I pressed on.

"You brought all these onto yourself!"

"Listen here, you piece of shit," he spoke in suppressed anger. "I did not kill anyone and you are barking up the wrong tree. You need to do your homework, son, before you get yourself hurt."

"Oh, I am way past hurt!"

"I don't think you know who you are messing with!"

"Just tell me why you had him killed."

"For the last time, I had nothing to do with that. He was my friend!"

With that, he slammed his fists on the table, gnarling at me but I held his gaze.

"I know guys like you – guys who think they can get away with anything…not this time pal, not this time!"

He took a deep breath, exhaled slowly and moved his hands from the table. He was clearly agitated but he looked like he was trying to flesh me out – find out what exactly I knew. He pushed himself against the back of the seat, took another deep breath and then leaned on the table.

"Listen to me," he said. "I might not be the most upstanding of citizens, but I am not a murderer!"

"Well, okay then."

I stood up, making to leave. I wanted to get him rattled – anything to get me a word, a concrete nugget out of him.

"I am filing my report in the morning – let the chips fall where they may. In the meantime, get yourself a good lawyer; you are going to need one."

"Hey, there is no need to be hasty," he called out.

I stopped in my tracks. Did I detect a note of fear?

"Please sit down, Mr. Chidi," he entreated.

I obliged. He cleared his throat, leaned towards me and whispered.

"You could ruin my business and my reputation with misinformation… and a libel suit against you would not restore my image and public trust," he conceded.

"Do I look like I give a fuck about that?" I replied. "You are complicit in human trafficking and murder – and you want to lecture me about an image?" I felt the 'animal' stir but I restrained myself.

"I thought you were after the truth. No?"

I did not respond. I could tell he was calculating his next move.

"I had nothing to do with it!" He implored.

"You can repeat that as many times as you want but you know the game is up. Texas is in flames – all your white buddies are either dead or on the run. But you, the trail of blood will end with you."

"I don't know what you are talking about but I could guide you in the right direction – one hand washing the other…on one condition."

"What?"

"You don't run the story before you have established the truth."

"What do you have for me?"

"You say you met William, so you must have also met Agnes…yes? You might want to look there."

"Are you saying that she killed Mehta?"

"She's the boss – lady."

"Why did she want him out?"

"He got soft."

"Why didn't she come for you? You were his partner."

He thought about it for a minute.

"Jack, I am not a fool. I know how to take care of myself. But let me offer you some … shall we say free advice?" He stood up, picked up his sports coat and continued, "I would be very careful if I were you… Should you so much as mention my name…"

"Is that a threat?"

"No, it's not a threat. It is a statement of fact and a word of friendly advice."

He lifted his right hand and snapped his fingers twice. Two burly men stood up from a booth behind us and came and stood next to him. I remembered them from his office. I had not seen them come in. Lidia's murderers!

He put on his coat, deliberately straightened it out by tagging at it and then, towering over the booth, he leaned towards me with a sinister smile. I could smell his breath.

"I have given you a lead, take it or leave it. But don't you ever come to me with this bullshit again – ever! Do we understand each other, Mr. Jack Chidi?"

Chapter Fifteen

I called Dipti early the next morning. She said that she and Saranya were headed to Kiambu Remand Center to visit her mother.

"How is she holding up?" I asked.

"Who? Saranya?"

"No, her mother, but well, Saranya too."

"Under the circumstances, she is doing okay. On Monday morning I will be moving to have the case dismissed, if you can make it. I'm sure she would like to see you."

I did not know how to tell her that her client's husband was probably knee – deep in an international sex ring and that perhaps his death had something to do with it.

"Hey, Dipti has she or anyone in the family ever mentioned anything to do with international job placements?"

"What do you mean?"

"Nothing, really, it's just that our investigation seems to be leading us to an illegal trade."

"What do you mean illegal trade – as in narcotics?"

Before I could answer, she asked me to hold on.

"Hello, Jack, this is Saranya"

"Hey, how are you?"

"I've been better but do you have some news for us?" she asked expectantly.

"Not much from this end – you are holding on okay?" I asked, trying to change the subject.

"You said that it had something to do with narcotics?"

"No, no. I was simply saying that there is a lead and we are following it closely."

"What kind of lead?"

"We are not sure how it ties to your father but let me ask you this: did you ever hear your father quarrel with someone over money, or anything?"

"Not really, why?"

"Did he ever argue with your mother about anything – anything to do with money or business…?"

She gasped loudly.

"So you also think she did it?" she asked.

"No…no, it's not what I mean. I am trying to understand the state of his finances – make sure he did not owe anyone any money…" I paused. "Can we meet? Some conversations are better held face to face."

"Sure. Where are you?"

"I'm in Dagoretti. We can meet at the Junction Mall. There's a small coffee shop as soon as you enter the mall, I forget the name but I'll head out there now."

"Okay. See you soon. I'll call you if I can't find it."

I decided to walk to the Junction since it was not far from my place. There was a nice little café that served up some of the best coffee in town and every now and then they hosted open mike nights for up and coming artists.

As soon as she walked in, I begun to regret calling this meet – but I needed all the help I could get to the bottom of the matter. It had to be done. She looked good in black skinny jeans, a white T-shirt and a jacket to match the jeans. Her hair was parted in the middle and braided into two long ropes that hang on each side of her head.

I pulled up a seat for her and she sat down, rubbed her hands together and cracked a smile. I walked to the other side of the table and made myself comfortable. She had a pleasant face, albeit the small scar across her right cheek and the small blackhead band aid on her nose – but her eyes – her eyes said she was still in mourning.

"Hey, where's Dipti?"

"Oh, she had to go to the office to pick up some documents."

"You look good."

"Thanks, Jack. And thank you for all you are doing for us. It's been a very rough time," she stated, her voice crackling like she was about to cry.

I felt bad for her – I had nothing to share, really, at least not with her at the moment. She needed answers, not conjecture.

"I know it's been tough for you and your mother, but we will get the bastards – you don't worry about that. It feels like we are closing in but I can't quite put my finger on it just yet."

"I appreciate what you are doing for my mother and me. I don't know how we will ever..."

"It's okay, Saranya. I'm just glad I can be of some help."

She pulled some strands of errant hair from her face and tucked them behind her ears.

We talked a little bit about her parents and how they doted on her. She seemed to have had a good upbringing, but like most young adults she had a rebellious period – "nothing crazy though" she had added with a little nervous laugh.

"Let me ask you this: you mentioned earlier that your father was working late and he seemed distant – when did this start?"

"I can't say exactly but it was recent."

"Of the people your father associated with; his business partners, friends – or even family, did any of them ever say or try to do something that was out of the ordinary – threaten, argue, fight?"

Before she could answer, a waiter came to our table and we ordered some coffee.

"No one comes to mind. His partners at MDE were also friends."

"You mean Mohali?"

"You know him?" Her voice, sharp and one register higher.

"Not personally – you don't seem to care for him," I stated, watching her closely.

"He just scares me – the way he looks at me sometimes." She shook her shoulders and let out a disapproving sound. "Ugh!"

Yeah, Mohali and women – even a friend's daughter! Could he have offed Mehta to get to his daughter? Okay, I was stretching, but I've known people to do as much for less.

"Did he spend a lot of time with your father?"

"I can't say for sure but one time he called my father an idiot. My mother said that Papa was not willing to relocate from his first store – you know, in Muindi Mbingu, but they finally convinced him to do it and he was not happy about it."

"You mean they forced him?" It was more of a statement.

The waiter brought our coffee, a welcome break I thought. She stirred some sugar into her coffee absent – mindedly.

"How was it with your parents?" I asked. "I mean, growing up with…"

"... with strict Indian parents?"

"Well, I guess we don't see strict parents as loving. We…"

"How was it with yours?" she turned it on me, quickly.

"I suppose all parents are the same," I said. "I am not even sure why I asked you. My mother was – is strict but in a nice way, I never knew my father, really. He died when I was really young."

"Did you ever wish for a different set of parents then?"

"Why?"

"Because then your life would be completely different – how did your father die?"

"He was stabbed to death over a hundred shillings he owed someone."

"I am so sorry. I did not mean to pry."

"It's okay, Saranya. That was a long time ago and like I said, I never knew the man."

I took a loud sip and I found Saranya staring at me.

"Are you okay, Jack?"

"Yes, why?"

"I don't know but it's like there is something bothering you. Is there anything I can do to help?"

"Oh, no no…you just take care of yourself and your mother," I hastened to say. I did not want to tell her that I was thinking that our fathers had died the same way and perhaps for the same reasons – kindred spirits.

"Saranya, at your house the other day your mother mentioned William, and of course I saw Mohali at her arraignment. What can you tell me about William?"

I saw her eyes widen. She started to say something then stopped. Then she let out a soft sigh. It was as though a dark cloud had suddenly descended on her. I knew she was in pain and I wanted to let her know that I was doing all I could to help them. "What is it?" I asked.

"Oh, it's nothing. I just want this to be over."

"Has Mohali or William tried to contact you?"

She was quiet, fidgety. "Just Mohali, he calls to check on me once in a while."

"What about William?" I asked after a little pause. I wanted her take on him.

She half – smiled and then bit her lower lip lightly. She looked beautiful and so delicately innocent.

"He called me from Texas to say *pole*," she replied.

"That was so nice of him."

"Nice? What is in…?" I checked myself. "Are you talking about William Burrows?"

"Yes, the oil tycoon – he was trying to get me a scholarship at Texas A&M but father said no."

"Oil tycoon? William…" I started to say and again checked myself.

Is this what he had told her?

"My father did not want me to go to Texas and leave him and mother all alone."

She shrugged her shoulders. I don't know what struck me more: the absolute innocence or the sheer irony. She obviously did not know William the way I did. If only she knew what this Texas tycoon really did for a living! For a moment I thought of telling her about the reality of William's life in Texas but I held back – for the time being.

Chapter Sixteen

I was back in my apartment thinking of the irony of William calling himself an Oil Man and offering Saranya a scholarship when Otieno called.

"Jack, I think I've got it!"

"What?"

"The girl on the news, you've seen her on TV! Saudi Arabia or some shit like!" he said excitedly.

"What about her?" I asked.

"Since we don't have Azani, this girl is our best bet and she is not afraid to talk."

He did not need to say any more. I called Dube and asked him if he could get me her address – someone in the CID had to know since she had filed a complaint with the authorities. Dube wanted to know why I was asking and so I explained.

He asked us to meet him at his office. I met up with Otieno and Jacob and we hit the road.

Dube was waiting for us and as soon as we pulled up, he came running downstairs and we took off for Uthiru. I sat in the back with him. He pulled out a folder and handed it to me.

"Her name is Caroline Musa," Dube started, looking over the file. "She is twenty two years old, lives with her parents, Mary and Katanga Musa, both teachers. Parents came home one day and she was gone. After many months of searching and even running a missing person in the newspapers, they gave her up for dead – until she showed up a few weeks ago."

It did not take us long to get there. After navigating through a muddy road past the Uthiru shopping center, we were greeted at the gate by a scrawny dog with a very loud bark. It ran alongside the car menacingly until we stopped in front of the house. As soon as we disembarked, it ran to the front door and stood guard, barking even louder.

An elderly woman opened the door and the dog stopped and lay down as if nothing had happened.

"Don't mind him" she said. "He is just trying to impress."

After shaking hands, we introduced ourselves and then she invited us in.

We gathered in her living room and as soon as we sat down, Dube explained, as best as he could, that we needed to speak to her daughter. It was possible that we were close to bringing the people who had forcefully detained her daughter to justice.

"Caroline will be protected should she choose to help us and you will have nothing to worry about."

Just as I was about to add to the conversation, the subject herself appeared in the doorway.

"It's Okay, Mama," she said as she walked to us and shook hands.

She was much smaller in person – at just under five feet but her gait was that of a grown woman. To look at her, one could not have believed or even imagined the horror that she had gone through.

"My name is Felix Dube, Special Agent with the CID. This here is Jack Chidi, that is Otieno and the other one is Jacob – all with the *Daily Grind*. We are investigating the recent spate of human trafficking and sex slavery in the country and we could use your help."

"I know Otieno; I really like your column."

"Thank you," Otieno smiled broadly, and fidgeted in his seat.

"Caroline, could you please tell us what happened to you – all of it or as much as you can. We need your help to get them – all of them."

She hesitated, eyeing us.

"I can assure you that from now on, you and your family will be assigned a security detail until this whole thing is over."

"Don't worry about that," she answered. "I'm not afraid anymore. There is nothing that anyone can do to me that I have not seen before. You only live and die once!"

Her voice had an echo of sadness that brought me to near tears.

"How did you get involved with…" Dube started to ask.

"I was promised a job as a babysitter for families who needed part – time nannies. I could keep my own hours. I had told my parents that I needed a job but they insisted I focus on school since they were providing for me, but I wanted to do more than just go to school and get a diploma – I needed real – life experience."

She paused and then continued.

"They were very convincing and they even introduced us to some girls who were already working – they seemed to be doing very well, so I signed up."

She told us that she did in fact work for a family in Karen, babysitting two little boys and helping them with homework. She did that for a few months and one day, a supervisor called her and told her there was an opportunity to work overseas for a short stint and that the pay was incredible – plus benefits. The supervisor told her that she would make all the arrangements for her travel – passport, air tickets and accommodation. It was too good to pass up and so within a few weeks she was flown to Saudi Arabia – working for a hotel magnate.

After a few nights, however, her Arabian host started demanding sex, saying that he had not paid for just a domestic worker. She refused and called her supervisor who, in a strange twist of events told her that it was okay – that it came with her contract. When she refused, the supervisor asked her to pay back all the money they had spent on her. The only way to do so was by fulfilling her contract which bound her to her employer for two years.

"Before she hung up, she said that she knew where my parents lived and that if I tried to run or call the police in Riyadh, they would kill my parents. I did not have any money, or anyone to contact because after that day, my employer took me down to a dungeon in his house and would only call me up when he needed entertainment – more often for himself but sometimes for his friends."

Tears welled up in her eyes and as they rolled down her cheeks, she casually wiped them off with her hand.

After a brief pause, Dube pulled out a stack of photos from his jacket and asked Caroline to look at them and see if she could identify any of them. I was a little surprised that he had not shown them to me but it did not matter now.

She stared at each one, carefully studying the faces before taking the next one. Otieno reached over and picked them up, looked at them and passed them to Jacob who in turn passed them on to me.

They were surveillance photos taken of several men, women, girls and buildings. We sat there going through photos until Caroline caught her breath after looking at one of them.

"This one," she said. "This is the main guy. He is the one who hired me."

Her hands were trembling as she returned the photo to Dube who then passed it on to me. It was Mohali.

Before we left the girl's home, Dube called his superior at the CID and requested security for Caroline and her mother. She was a potential witness for the prosecution.

"I wonder why the bad guys have not tried to silence her," Otieno mused.

"The publicity she is getting has given her some protection," Dube answered. "She is a celebrity of sorts, but that will not hold for long so we will have a security detail for her and her family until we get these bastards."

From Dube I knew that arrests would follow soon. But these would merely be in connection with the Kenyan end of the sex trade. I felt like I had been running all over the place only to end up in the same spot – with Mohali right in the thick of it. That bugger was guilty as sin.

He was linked to Lidia, Azani, Logic Placements and now Caroline. He was Mehta's silent partner at the pharmacy. All these but no tangible lead to the murder. He had even thrown in that line about Agnes and the lot only after he knew they were either dead or under arrest. But I was closing in on him.

Later, acting on an impulse, I called Dube again: "Do you think that Mohali might try to leave the country? The walls are closing in on him."

"I already have eyes on him," he assured me.

Chapter Seventeen

I was back at the office and had just sat down at my desk when my phone rang. I pulled it out of my pocket and looked at the number. I did not recognize it except that the call was a local number.

"Hello," I answered.

The beeping sound alerted me to a dropped call. I placed it on the desk and turned on my desktop computer. I remembered that I had not called Irene as promised. So I dialed her number – I knew it was going to be late in Texas but I needed to hear her voice and assure her that I had made it in safely.

There was no answer and I waited for voicemail to pick up but an incoming call buzzed in and I quickly answered it, thinking that she had seen my missed call and hit me back.

"Hi stranger," I said, trying to be cute.

There was a little bit of silence and some accompanying static.

"Yes, my friend. How are you?"

It was a female voice and it sounded eerily familiar but it was not Irene.

"Hello, who is this?"

"Oh, come on now, Jack. You disappoint me. You want to say you don't remember me at all? I helped you with a little blue..."

"Agnes!" I almost screamed out in surprise.

I pulled the phone from my ear and looked at it. She was calling from a local number which meant she was in the country.

"Oh, I remember you…"

"Well, I understand that you are interested in me, right? So I thought I might visit you and see what it is that you want from me."

My lips dried up and I looked around the office – as if trying to make sure I was safe.

"Who told you that?"

"Come on now, Jack."

"And how did you get my number?"

"You left someone behind in Texas; a certain lady – she was quite a lovely woman."

I felt my heart sink.

"What do you mean was?"

"Jack, Jack, Jack… You know how these things work." She paused and then added, "You didn't think we would let you get away with what you have done, did you?"

She let out a short but forced laugh and then hung up.

I felt light – headed as I dialed Irene's number again. It rang a few times and then someone picked it up.

"Hello, Irene?" I called out, almost relieved.

The voice on the other side was not Irene. It was a man who identified himself as Special Agent Mark Palmer, from the Houston Police Department.

"My name is Jack Chidi, with the *Daily Grind* in Nairobi …a paper in Kenya."

He wanted to know my connection to Irene. I told him we were good friends and that I had spent two nights in her house.

"What was the nature of your visit to Texas?"

"What is this about?" I asked.

"There was a break – in and apparently we now have a missing person. You wouldn't know anything about that would you?"

"No, when I left she was fine. Have you checked with her husband?"

"Yes…he had not heard from her in weeks. I would like to ask you a few questions, if that's ok with you."

"Sure, sure, but what happened to her, detective?" I asked.

"Someone seems to have been very angry at her by the look of things."

I felt weak at the knees. Tears would not come. If what he was saying was true, my Irene was gone and I was under the famous umbrella of suspicion.

I felt the "animal" stir deep inside me. The ball game had changed completely – fuck all this bullshit!

"About your contact…?"

"I will have to get back to you on that."

I hang up the phone and wiped the sweat from my palms.

My heart was pounding and I felt a little light headed but I had enough presence of mind to call Dube to tell him that Agnes, and possibly William, was in the country and that they were going for broke. I did not tell him about Irene. I did not want him thinking that I was hell bent on revenge.

Otieno was having a late breakfast at Anne's Butchery of all places when I caught up with him the next morning. I ordered two eggs and three sausages and when they came, I dug right in. It was then I realized that I had missed dinner altogether the night before.

"I'm sorry about Irene," Otieno said sincerely.

"I know, man. It's tough. I keep losing …"

"Don't you go blaming yourself man, it's not your fault."

I wanted to believe him but the fact was that had it not been for me, she would still be alive and well.

"But you said that she's just missing...they have not concluded anything yet. These American CSI types – they comb through everything. I'm sure they will find her."

"I know, but still, I can't help but think she is gone."

I took a small bite of my sausage, still thinking of Irene when it hit me. I put down my fork and hurriedly pulled out my phone. I dialed Dale's number. He could check it out for me but he had to be careful. The phone rang once and then a voice advised that the number was no longer in service!

"I can't even get a break!" I yelled out and just before Otieno could say anything, my phone rang and I grabbed at it.

"Hello!"

It was Dube. He had lost the trace on Mohali.

"What?"

"He was able to shake my men. I think they followed the wrong car from his house."

"Where did they lose him?"

"Mombasa Road, but..."

"He is headed for the airport!" I exclaimed.

"He never made it there. We don't know where he is." Dube sounded a little exasperated. "We are now chasing ghosts," he added.

"You have a trace on his cell phone, credit cards..."

"Hey, Jack, dude is off the grid, for now at least. But we will track him down."

I was about to remind him that I had asked him to keep a twenty four hour surveillance on the man but decided against it. What good would it do?

"Something is way off," Dube said. "It's like he was tipped off."

"One of yours?"

"Oh, hell no! But I'm sure he suspected something – these guys are vigilant, that's how they stay ahead of the game."

"Agnes did mention that somebody told her that I was interested in her – but in fact it was Mohali who pointed me in her direction – he thinks she put the hit out on Mehta, so I'm sure he is on edge."

"Sounds like they are pointing fingers at each other–I think it's going to get ugly very quickly. We are keeping an eye on Saranya, just in case they come for the family. They will not stop until they have put a lid on this."

Otieno and I talked for a little while after Dube's call. It had already turned ugly and I was going to fight back with everything I had in me. It was time to push the envelope and let the shit fall where it may. It was good to know he was hanging with me all the way. I said so to him as we boarded a *matatu* to the city center.

Jacob picked us up near Khoja Mosque. We decided to go back to the pharmacy and see what we could shake up. We needed a break. Any break would do – I had to get these guys – for Irene, for Mehta and for me!

We drove in silence. I had a lot on my mind. How would I ever reconcile it to myself if indeed they had killed Irene?I should have never taken Azani to Irene's house – or better still, I should never have gotten involved with her at all. The only way they could have known about Irene was through Azani who I now knew was as good as dead. There was no way they were going to let her off scot – free with all the damning information she had – no loose ends.

Just before we joined Limuru Road, I got a call from Solomon – he had just spotted Mohali walking into Fig Tree Hotel just as he was getting ready to leave. He had seen him alight from a cab – and yes, he was alone.

"So that's how he lost his tail." I smiled at the simple but clever ploy. "We are just round the corner. Are you still at the Fig?"

"Yeah, but I have a business meeting in like fifteen minutes across town. He looks like he is meeting someone."

"Okay, we will be right up…"

"Ooo, looks like whoever he was waiting on has just arrived… damn, she's one fine lady!"

"Is it an Asian – looking woman?" I asked.

"Oops. She just left. Not the right one…"

"Okay, man, stay focused, we'll be right up."

I relayed the message to Otieno and Jacob and then called Dube and told him we were on the way to the Fig Tree.

"Can you stall him?" he asked. "I'll be there in less than fifteen minutes. I don't care if you pin him to the floor. We have to stop the bloodshed before it starts."

"What's the plan?" Otieno asked after I put the phone down.

"Just keep him there. Dube will take him in for questioning."

"So we just walk in and entertain him?"

"It's all I have. There is no way he is going to have us taken out in public."

Solomon was waiting at the far end of the lobby, pretending to read a newspaper and as soon as we walked in, he called us over. He wanted to know if he could do anything to help.

"No, man, I appreciate it though. We got this. Besides,

Dube is on his way."

My heart was pounding heavily from the anticipation but I knew I also had to keep my wits about me. One wrong move and the whole thing would be a bust. The answers we sought were here – or coming to us!

After Solomon left, Otieno, Jacob and I walked to the patio bar away from the entrance, sat down and ordered some coffee. From here we could see anyone walking in and out of the lounge. I hoped Dube would get here soon before Mohali decided to leave and I had to tackle him. He usually had two bodyguards waiting in the shadows – but not this time, he had come in alone – but that did not mean that they would not show up.

About five minutes in, the front doors slid open and a woman walked in. She was wearing one of those huge sombrero hats, pulled down her face and the only thing I could make out was her neck. She had a red skirt on that hugged her tightly around the waist, black high heels and a small purse that she held tightly under her arm. She walked across the far end of the bar and into the lounge.

"Did you see that?" Otieno asked.

"You think that's who he's meeting?"

"She could be anyone. All we want right now is that Mohali does not get out."

I looked at the time. Dube should be here anytime now.

Almost three minutes after she had walked in, I saw her and Mohali walking towards the back of the hotel. They were leaving using the back exit. There was no way I was going to let him get away. I jumped from my bar stool and followed them.

The back door was ajar when I got there. I leaned against

the right wall and peeked out. I could see Mohali standing about fifteen meters away, near a dumpster. I could not see the woman but I could see the brim of her sombrero and then her hands would come into view and then disappear. I could not make out all the words that spilled over from their animated conversation but I caught a good part of it.

I heard her say something about money and getting the hell out of town to which he retorted that she was in more danger now than in Texas…

"You were supposed to take care of it…I do not owe…but this is no longer…you are on your own."

He was clearly angry with her.

"No! I helped you all build…I refuse to be treated like a piece…! You will pay me my money!" she shouted before catching herself.

Mohali was irate.

"You are compromised! I don't owe you shit! Go ask Agnes for your money! But I'm warning you, you better not…"

"I'm the one who told William where to find him. I was protecting you, William and Agnes. You owe me that much."

"You told him everything…"

"No, I did not. But somebody is going to pay me!"

"Or what?"

I felt some one tap me on the shoulder. Startled, I spun around with my right hand cocked ready to lash out.

"Hey, what are you doing?"

It was the chef, a stoutly built black man in a white uniform and hair net. I tried to shush him but he was not having it. I mentioned that I was with the press.

"I don't care. That door is for employees only!" He said it

even louder pointing to a sign that said the same.

I looked outside. Mohali and the woman were staring at me. The woman had now tipped her sombrero hat backwards so it no longer covered her face. It was Azani!

I saw Mohali reach behind his back. I knew he was going for a gun. I jumped backwards, knocking the chef over. I heard the bang and almost instantaneously the bullet slammed the door jamb, inches from my head and I felt the splinters slam my face and neck. I tripped over the prostrate chef but I managed to scramble to my feet and run into the kitchen.

I sprinted past waiters and waitresses, some of who had stood still trying to figure out what the hell was going on. Several patrons scampered out of the restaurant screaming. I did not know if Mohali was in pursuit or not. I ran across the patio, and slid head first onto the cement floor and under the table where I had left Otieno and Jacob.

All of a sudden the screaming stopped. I looked up from under the table and saw detective Dube and Special Agent Njoki, guns trained towards the direction I had just come from. I traced my eyes slowly and saw Mohali, gun in hand with Azani standing next to him.

"Ok, Mohali. My name is Detective Dube. I am with the CID. Put down your weapon."

"I can't do that," Mohali answered. He looked despondent, almost desperate.

"Do as he says." Njoki barked and pulled the hammer back.

Azani, who was clutching her purse tightly with her left hand, placed her right hand over it and ever so slowly started to unzip it.

"I would not do that if I were you." Dube told her. "Put

that gun on the ground now!"

Mohali looked around and suddenly raised his gun to his head but before he could pull the trigger, Dube shot him once. The impact pushed him backwards but he maintained his balance. He brought the gun up one more time. Dube shot him again. I saw him crumble to the ground. The gun dropped from his fingers.

Azani looked at it once, and then at Dube and Njoki – "please don't do it" I whispered to myself.

"Don't even think about it. Drop that purse and put your hands up in the air!"

She looked at Mohali, who was on the ground writhing in pain and decided to give herself up. He was lucky that Dube had shot him once in the shoulder and the second time on the knee. Njoki and Dube handcuffed them. I walked over to where Azani was being held.

"So you were in this all along?"

She did not answer me.

"And to think I went all that way to save you!"

"Save me?" She let out a small laugh, her eyes defiant, not like the scared girl I had saved from Stocky and The Farm.

"So where do you feature in all this?" I asked. "What about your friend Lidia?"

"She was not my friend; I was just helping her find work."

"So, you recruited the girls. What about the tears? Texas, remember?"

She looked away and shook her head defiantly. "I had to find out what you knew."

"Wow! You are quite the actress," I said.

She looked at me and smiled at me – mockingly.

"Oscar – winning performance," I added sarcastically, my

oice quivering in anger.

"Why were you with Stocky if you are part of the…?"

She was quiet for a second – and for that one brief moment she looked hurt, as if she understood that she too was expendable.

Her voice had lost the earlier bravado as she said, "I just do what I can to survive!"

She then turned away from me just as Dube walked up to us.

"Jack, I really have to get this guy attended to. They both have a lot of questions to answer and believe me they will – like I said, there's going to be no bloodbath in my city."

I knew the answers would come shortly but there was no waiting. It was time to rattle the cage some more.

Chapter Eighteen

Otieno and Jacob were waiting in the car for me. For two guys who had seen most of the action, they tried to play it off but I could tell they were shaken. Jacob said that after they heard the gunshot, they had ducked under the table to call the police but then they saw Felix and Njoki on the scene. Otieno did not try any of his usual jokes but we were all safe, for now.

I was still shaken up and my hands were trembling.

We decided to stop by MDE. Within minutes Jacob pulled up and parked by the roadside next to the pharmacy. I asked him to keep the motor running while Otieno and I paid Olivia a visit.

There was no one in the reception area and so I rung the small bell at the edge of the counter. The sound reverberated across the empty room with an annoying sharpness but it did the trick. I heard a door open and the click – clack of high heels coming towards us. It was Olivia.

"What can I do for you today?" she asked.

She then cocked her head to the side and smiled.

"You can start by telling us where William and Agnes are staying."

"Who?"

"You know damn well who I'm talking about!" I shouted.

"No, I don't."

"Let me repeat: Agnes, Burrows or William…where are they?"

She shook her head. I did not have time to pussyfoot with her.

"We know about this pharmacy, about William, Mohali, Agnes, Roger...all the girls being sent out... the whole operation so you had better..."

"Whoa! Whoa! Whoa!" She raised her hands in the air but the fake smile was gone. "What the fuck are you talking about?"

"Stop playing dumb, I have enough on you to get you put away for involvement in sex – trafficking and, God forbid, murder!"

"Excuse me! I had nothing to do with it," she shot back angrily and then stopped herself as if she had just realized the implications of her denial. "I would like you to leave right now!"

"Listen, Ms. Jones. You had better start talking to me, a journalist, unless you would rather talk to the police."

Her eyes welled up and her face changed color.

Otieno walked closer to her and handed her a handkerchief which she took and dabbed the tears from the corner of her eyes.

"What's your name again – we were not properly introduced?" He asked, in a friendly tone. "My name is Otieno."

"Olivia. Olivia Jones."

"Well, Olivia. Have you ever been to a Kenyan jail?"

"No."

"And you don't want to, trust me on this one."

"But I can't go to jail. I did not do anything wrong."

"Of course you didn't but the police don't like to hear that. You tell us all you know and we will help you when they come for you. Can we go to your office and sit down?" he asked her as, with his signature smile, he pulled her aside.

He was so convincing that I found myself ready to confess my sins. She led us down the corridor and into her office.

"So how long have you worked here?" Otieno asked as soon as she had composed herself behind her desk.

I sat to her right and Otieno sat on the left corner of the desk just in front of her.

"Well, not long, about five years."

"How did you get started?" Otieno asked with the patience of a saint.

She hesitated and then smiled sheepishly. I thought she was stalling for time, trying to find a way out.

"Olivia," I interjected impatiently, "you better start talking or else we are no longer bound to the promises we have made to you."

"I was hired through Roger."

"Roger Caldwell?"

"Yes, we were lovers – well he was a regular, in New York and when he was transferred to Texas, he took me with him. And then we ended up here." She started to sob. "I trusted him and I did what he asked me to do."

I looked at Otieno and then back to her.

"You mean to say that you were…?"

"I ran away from home and moved to New York with a friend. We did not know anyone and we found ourselves desperate and somehow we were lured into…into the bad life and then eventually we were turning tricks for this guy – a pimp, really, in New York and that's how I met Roger. He was good to me. He said he had a friend who owed him a favor and that's how I ended up here."

She did not put it that way but threats of taking her back to the streets were enough to keep her faithful and loyal to him.

193

Did she know that her Mr. Wonderful was dead? If she did, she did not show it. I thought I should tell her to break her loyalty to a has – been, and for me to see her reaction to the news.

"When is the last time you saw Roger?" I asked.

"It's been a while. He usually calls me when he is coming over to my place – at least once a month, you know, to, eh, visit." She turned her eyes to the floor. Yeah, he was still coming to collect favors whenever he felt like it. "He is good to me." She added as an afterthought that would make it all seem okay.

"You are in some serious trouble Olivia."

"Roger will take care of it, he always does." She sobbed.

"I don't know how to tell you this but Roger is dead."

She looked at me and for a second it was as if nothing had registered.

"We are still close…what? What did you just say?"

"Roger is dead. They shot him last week."

"Oh, my God!" She gasped. "That's why I have not heard from him all week!" She clasped her hands on her mouth, her eyes widened and then tears begun to flow down her cheeks.

"Who killed him?" she whispered between heaves of air.

"These are bad people and they will kill anyone who they think is…"

"Who killed him?"

She then started crying, heaving her shoulders violently with every breadth. We let her bawl for a while and then Otieno held her.

"Olivia, help us help you. Tell us everything you know about…who killed Mr. Mehta? Remember, you might be next and we might not be able to help you if…"

"I honestly don't know."

"Did you see anyone with Mehta who looked suspicious, or hear anything out of the ordinary?"

"Well, not really, but I heard him argue with someone on the phone."

"Who was it?"

"I could not tell."

"And what did they argue about?"

"All I heard him saying was that whoever it was, needed to leave her alone, that if it did not stop he was going to take action."

"Did he say what kind of action?" I was beginning to get a picture but it was blurry.

"He just said he would bring the whole operation down."

"What operation? How?"

"He just kept shouting on the phone, which surprised me because he was always so laid back. I knew something was..."

"What did he say...?"

"...For them to leave her alone or he would take action, and then he was quiet and the last thing he said was: '*over my dead body.*' After that he became very distraught and paranoid – always locking his door and asking if I had seen any strangers hanging around."

The blurry picture was getting some color on the edges. Mehta and the mystery caller were fighting over a woman and Mehta had threatened to expose their whole operation. A woman and threats of exposure had signed his death warrant and he knew it.

"Tell me, who calls the shots?"

She hesitated just a tad and then said, "Agnes, she is the boss, then William, Roger, Mohali and then..."

"Agnes, from Texas?" I looked at Otieno and he was just as puzzled. He was about to say something when we heard the door creak.

"Don't answer any more questions!" A huge voice thundered from the doorway.

I turned around quickly to see Man – child standing by the doorway, gun in hand. His hair was pulled back into a small pony tail which made him look more like a school – boy than a gangster.

"You, move over to the side."

I was not sure who he was referring to so I moved. Otieno was looking at him with a bemused smile on his face but I hoped he was taking him seriously.

"No tricks! Just do as I say and no one gets hurt."

He reached into his pocket, pulled out a phone and dialed a number. After a few seconds he mumbled something into it and then listened.

He turned and looked at us and continued talking on the phone.

"Yes…both of them…yes, she was talking…no, I'm not sure she told them anything… Okay, I'll send her on her way."

He listened for a while and then raised his gun and pointed it at Olivia.

"You, you are done here!"

She stood up, picked up her handbag and turned to walk out. I don't remember hearing the blast. All I saw was her body buckle then slump, almost slowly to the floor. I ducked under the desk.

"Hey, man, don't shoot!" It was Otieno. "What the hell, man, don't shoot!"

"It's your lucky day, bitches! He wants you alive or else I would have done you in."

"Who?"

"You'll soon find out. Get up on your feet – both of you, now! We are going for a ride."

He pointed his gun at me and then Otieno.

"I ought to kill one of you though – makes it easier to transport."

I tried to say something but no sound came. He motioned us with a flick of the gun to walk towards the door and he followed us out. I was walking in front of Otieno and once outside I turned to signal Jacob for help. He was nowhere to be found and something told me right away that Man – child had something to do with it.

Man – child pointed to a black Mitsubishi Gallant parked in the back. As we walked towards it, I remembered the car that had almost run me over. This was it! I turned to look at Man – child. How long had this fool been tracking me down?

Otieno was ordered in the trunk and after he had folded himself into a ball, Man – child closed the trunk. He then pushed me into the driver's side, walked to the front passenger side and once inside he handed me the keys.

"Just drive and don't try anything stupid."

He pulled some gum from his pocket and started chewing, his gun pointing directly at me. We were now on Limuru Road headed back to the city. At the Old Nation roundabout, we cut across and headed to Uhuru Highway and soon we joined the traffic headed towards Westlands.

"Where are you taking us?" I asked just to keep him talking.

"Just drive, Newspaper man. You know you are a pain in the ass, right?" He chuckled, almost to himself. "If it was up to me, I would have given it to you right there and then – Pow! Pow! One each."

The only person who had called me that was Agnes. It was clear to me that wherever we were being taken to, we would not be coming back alive.

"So are you part of it or are you just a pawn?" I asked.

"Hey! I'm no one's pawn. I carry my own weight." He looked at himself as if he had doubts and then at me. "Are you trying to make fun of me, you bloody fool?" He raised his gun and placed it on my temple. "I can shoot you right now!"

"Now, now, just calm down. I was just asking if…"

"You need to shut the fuck up!"

He chewed on his gum loudly as he looked from side to side to see as if he was expecting something to happen. Was he nervous? I decided to ignore him for a while and focus on trying to find a way out. After a little ways, he pointed to the left turn that was coming up. I did not catch the street name but after a series of lefts and rights, we made it to Valley Arcade and onto Gitanga Road.

We were headed to Roger's house!

I decided to prod him again.

"Why don't you let us go?"

He stared at me for a long time. I could feel his eyes burning the side of my face – the same way a dog looks at a piece of meat that his master will not let him have.

"Just do as I tell you!" he snarled at me.

He lifted up his gun again as if to remind me he was still in charge.

"You don't have to do this, you know."

"You talk too much." He poked me hard in the ribs with the gun. "Bloody fool! I can't wait to shut you up!"

He jabbed me again with the gun and this time I felt a sharp pain shoot up my right side.

Man – child had me park directly behind the garage, hidden under a huge Jacaranda tree. He grabbed the keys from the ignition as soon as the car came to a stop and then ordered me to get out and help Otieno get out of the trunk.

"We are at Roger's house," I whispered to Otieno.

"Who else is here?" he asked, trying to stretch out his back and his legs.

Man – child was not happy with our whispering. "Hey! Let's go! Get in there!"

He handed Otieno a key and asked him to open the garage door and we walked in.

"I have to use the bathroom." I said as soon as the door closed behind us.

He pointed to the corner.

"I need some privacy. It's a number two."

"I don't give a damn which number! If I see you trying anything funny, I will shoot you both. I don't have time for this." He pulled out his phone and dialed a number.

"We are here." he said and hung up.

He asked us to sit down on the floor while he pulled out an old dining room chair and sat down, his legs barely touching the floor... He reached into his pockets, pulled out a joint and lit it up. The little bugger was getting high right in front of us. But that was the least of our worries.

I looked at Otieno, trying to communicate to him that any chance we had was between now and when the boss came to the scene. I was not sure what he was trying to tell me by rubbing his eyes and then blinking rapidly but I hoped that it meant that we were on the same page.

I looked around the garage. It was well organized – blue storage boxes neatly piled one on top of the other. To the left, hanging on the wall, gardening tools, an electric hedge trimmer, a push mower and an old bicycle – a black mamba complete with the small dynamo that generated power for the flashlight mounted on the handle bar.

I heard a car pull up in the driveway and moments later the garage doors opened. For a few seconds all we could see was a silhouette of what appeared to be a tall man.

He walked over to where we were and stood in front of us with his hands in his pockets.

"I see Dave here has made you quite comfortable." He said it casually.

William wore a safari hat with wildlife logo in the front and straps hanging to the sides. For a top he wore one of those *kente* cloth shirts over denim jeans and beige walking shoes. Without knowing what he did for a living, he would have passed for just another casual tourist.

Up close and in person, he had a soft face – almost polite. He removed his hat and handed it over to Man – child. He had a lot of hair on his head but I noticed there was a mismatch – he was wearing a toupee! He must have seen me staring at it or he was self – conscious for he turned and made a few adjustments to the rug before he sat down on the seat Man – child had been using.

"Well, Jack Chidi. You've been quite a pain in my ass," he said, smiling unaffectedly.

"I'm just doing my job," I answered without rancor.

"Do you know how much money you have cost me? Do you have any idea?" His calm demeanor was betrayed by a tremor in his voice.

"Unintended consequences of my investigation," I said, shrugging my shoulders.

He let out a huge laugh, rocking himself back and forth in the chair.

"Unintended consequences, he says," he repeated as he looked at Man – child who stood there stoically, gun and hat in hand.

"So you were friends with Mr. Mehta, were you?" I asked after the laughter had waned.

I had to keep him talking – stalling for time and hoping for an opening – the first one that came my way.

"Ah, fucking Mehta. What an Indian fool! Sorry, Dave, but I have said this before; Indians are as cowardly and greedy as Africans are lazy. You all expect to ride on someone's back even for things you can do for yourselves – always trying to take advantage of someone's philanthropy."

"You call yourself a philanthropist?" Otieno jumped in.

"What the fuck do you think?" William responded, his nostrils flaring up and his eyes growing wide. "You have it all wrong. I am a people person – a businessman if you will. I create opportunities for employment. You know that, Mr. Jack Chidi, don't you?" He winked at me.

"Prostitution and sex – parties are hardly legitimate business ventures."

"Bullshit, I provide services that people want!" he boasted.

"These girls are tricked into thinking that they are getting legitimate jobs…"

"They come to us because they are tired of this god –

orsaken life – what is wrong with you Africans? All self – righteous BS but living in shit holes waiting for some white motherfucker to bail you out! No one forces them to sign contracts and no one forces them to have sex. They do it because of the money. It's all about the money!"

He was frothing again. I stood up.

"Just tell me why you killed Mehta."

"Well, not that you need to know but he was letting the personal get in the way of business. I don't like that at all – it gets in the way of good decisions and trust." He took two steps towards me and then stopped. "You see, trust is the engine of much of what we do," he continued with an air of superiority. "Without it, we cannot function. So what would you do if you cannot trust your associate? Mmh? What would you do?"

Before I could respond, Man – child's phone rang. He pulled out his phone and answered it. He listened for a few seconds and then handed it to William.

"Hello…oh, yes, we are waiting on Mohali…no not everything is as planned…" He listened, and then added, "No, no, he should be here by now…no he will show…yes, he sounded scared as usual but he'll be here…yes, Ma'am."

I wondered when he had talked to Mohali. That was impossible! Mohali could not have possibly overpowered Dube, not with a shattered kneecap. Unless, somehow, Azani had managed to do it – she had proved to be quite resourceful.

He tossed the phone back to Man – child.

He flashed a smile and then indulgently asked, "Aah, where were we?"

"You were telling us why Mehta had to die…about trust. But you could have done all that without him."

Just then someone opened the garage door and walked in and as soon as the light hit her, I recognized Agnes. She moved slowly, deliberately. I could tell, even with a smile caressing her lips, that she was angry – irritably angry!

"We meet again, Jack. You have become quite a pest." She turned to look at Otieno and then back at me. "Did you tell him what happens to your friends?"

I did not answer.

She walked over to William and faced him. He looked uncomfortable – he no longer had the hubris he had displayed just a few minutes ago.

"How long before Mohali gets here?" she asked him impatiently. She looked at her watch and then pointed a finger at William, "You are all incompetent fucks! But you better clean this shit up…"

"Dave and I can…we will take care of it…" William started to say.

"Just like he did, huh? Is that what Dave did, in his garage where his wife and child could find him?" She was really pissed off.

Man – child fidgeted, cleared his voice and said: "I'm not the one who killed him!"

Agnes turned to Man – child: "What did you just say?"

"I didn't kill him. I found him like that…"

"Oh, shut the fuck up!" Williams said in a slightly desperate tone.

Man – child stared at Williams defiantly but did not say another word. Agnes reached in her purse and I thought she was getting a gun but instead she pulled out a pack of cigarettes and pulled one out, slowly. She lit it and turned to William.

"I don't know why he is denying it…" William tried to say.

She put her hand up in his face.

"I don't give a fuck! You are responsible for all this shit! I warned you about messing with her – this is not America, but no! You just could not keep it in your pants!"

Her voice tailed off and she was quiet for a minute. She looked at her wristwatch and muttered under her breath – something about incompetence.

"Do not fuck this up!" she added in a cold steely voice.

Then she pointed a long finger at William but changed her mind and started to walk out.

"Hey, Agnes," I called out. "It's over!"

She stopped and turned towards me.

"It's over when I say it is over!" she retorted, her voice loaded with contempt.

She gave me a long look, half smiled and turned to William. She stared him down and he held her gaze for a second before looking away, guiltily. He started to say something but she lifted her hand to stop him and then walked away.

At the door she stomped on her cigarette and turned to look at William again.

"Get rid of them…we have a lot to sort out."

Then we heard a car start and drive off.

William let out a huge sigh and then forced a smile to his lips. He walked to the door as if to make sure she was gone and then came back to where we were.

"Women!" he said, shaking his head from side to side. "We used to be friends, you know, close friends – a long time ago. But I moved on – fell in love with someone else…"

He said all that as if he was thinking aloud, trying to recover his wounded pride.

"Who was she talking about?" I asked just to make sure I had it right.

He smiled and cocked his head to his side.

"Saranya," he sighed out her name.

"As in Saranya Mehta?" I asked in surprise. This was not what I expected. The thought had never even come to my mind.

"Yes, Saranya Mehta," he admitted and confirmed with something like relief in his tired voice; "A forbidden kind of love...her father would have none of it. Understandable, but I knew once he got to know me better, he would come around. He just made the mistake of threatening the entire operation...That could not be ..."

"So you killed the father so that you could get at the daughter?" Otieno chimed in.

Suddenly, as if he had woken from wherever his wounded pride had taken him, he turned and looked at Man – child, who fidgeted on his feet.

"You told me you took care of it, you little fuck!" he shouted.

Man – child stood his ground but he seemed a little nervous.

"Don't insult me!" he answered, his voice trembling. "You wanted him dead and you were with him that night. You killed him and now you're trying to set me up."

William was about to lash out at Man – child but he caught himself. He realized he was cornered, almost defeated plus Man – Child still had his gun in hand.

"I didn't kill Mehta," he said shaking his head.

Something was wrong here.

"And I didn't kill him," replied Man – child. "So, if neither of us killed him, then who did? Mohali?"

That was what we all wanted to know and for a moment my heart stood still as I waited to get confirmation. But it was not forthcoming.

"What does it matter anyway?" William shrugged instead. "This is where we are…!"

And where is that? I wanted to ask in frustration. We were so near, yet so far away from what we had been after.

William looked at his watch and cursed: "Where the fuck is this imbecile?"

He started walking towards Man – child and suddenly we heard a car drive up and stop abruptly. Car doors slammed shut and we heard the sound of feet running – and then silence. William stopped and turned to face the garage door, the smile of relief on his face now gone.

"What the hell is that?" he asked, snapping his fingers at Man – child who sprang into action. He tiptoed to the garage door and walked out towards the main house. It got quiet again for a minute or so. Then a burst of gunfire broke the silence. I heard someone scream and then more shots rang out. I saw William aim for the florescent light in the garage. Then I heard more shots just as the room went dark. I jumped behind a stack of boxes, followed closely by Otieno. Two more shots rang out and I heard the loud thwacks as the bullets hit the boxes near where we were. I curled up and braced myself, waiting for the pain to come.

And then the shooting stopped and I heard a familiar voice calling my name from a distance. It was Felix Dube.

"Jack! Is everything okay in there?"

I peered out and saw flashlight beams walking towards us.

"Jack, are you okay in there?"

It was our rescue but we stayed down, completely depleted.

Chapter Nineteen

After a while, the light beams focused on us.

"Did you get him?" I asked as I slowly got up.

"We got one. There's one on the loose but we will pick him up soon, I have my guys on his trail. He can't get far."

"How about Agnes?" I asked expectantly.

"She must have left before we got here but how long and how far do they think they can run – a white man and a white woman?"

He smiled knowingly.

I was about to tell him that she was not exactly white – but it would not make a difference; she looked more white than Asian and that made her white.

"How did you know where to find us?" I asked him as we walked out.

"Mohali told me – they called him just as we sat down at the station for a talk."

I thanked Dube and then I remembered Jacob. I pulled out my phone and called his number. After a few rings he answered – he sounded like he had a cold.

"Hey, man, you okay?" I asked.

"Yeah, how about you guys?"

"We're okay. But you don't sound too good."

He coughed and then said, coyly, "I waiting for you guys when all of a sudden I was blindsided by some little … "

Man – child!

"I thought as much," I said to Jacob. "But don't you worry, man. We'll catch up tomorrow. You just get some rest, eh?"

We walked past Man – child, who was prostrate on the driveway – he had been shot twice in the chest. In death he looked even more like a little boy and not the cold blooded killer that he was.

*****

The next morning, I called Dube for an update. His team had combed through the neighborhood, woken up residents, checked their homes and storage sheds, garages and flower beds, and even under children's playground sets but William was nowhere to be found. How far could a tall, skinny white man and a lovely white woman go on foot without being detected in a sea of blackness?

An APB was out on them. There were roadblocks in and out of the city, with every cop on the beat directed to find them, quietly of course – tourist dollars were still needed in the country. We were slowly closing in on them but every turn seemed to reveal a different twist. It was clear that William had outsmarted and outmaneuvered us all. He had taken Mehta out and had hoped to have Dave or Mohali take the fall – just so he could have his daughter! And now he had gotten away.

I called Otieno. He sounded sleepy but he tried to play it off by attempting to sound awake. I told him that I was headed to Anne's for breakfast and asked him to join me.

I did not wait long for Otieno to come. He was still not wide awake yet but he still had that smile on his face.

"So what did you think of William and Saranya?" I asked him as soon as he sat down and ordered a tall glass of milk and quarter loaf of bread. I was having black tea and *mandazi* myself.

"I think he was just making up all that shit. First of all, she is way too young for him, and secondly, Indians usually stick to their kind."

"Agreed! But let's assume that he loves her but her father is objecting, what would he do? Eliminate him, bide his time to smooth talk her and voila! She's all his."

"Knowing what kind of man he is, no father would want William around their daughter – Indian or not."

"We still have to find him."

Otieno took a bite of the half – loaf, slurped on his milk and then chewed noisily.

I took one bite of my *mandazi* and then leapt to my feet.

"Yo! Let's roll!" I thundered to Otieno.

"Easy there, cowboy, I have to finish my…"

"There is not time! Get Jacob, quick!"

I called Dube and told him that we were heading out to the Mehta residence. When I told him why, he couldn't wait to get on the way. Yet after I was done, he admonished me for not telling him about William's claims on Saranya earlier. But his tone was almost one of relief.

"I'm on my way," he confirmed. "But let's meet at the Tigoni Police Station. Don't go in without me! It's dangerous!"

Chapter Twenty

"Man, that little bugger really did you in!" Otieno said as soon as Jacob picked us up. His nose was bandaged with thick gauze. His left eye was also a little puffed up but he had not sustained any life – threatening injury. Knowing Man – child, Jacob was lucky to have escaped with his life.

"Yeah, but wait until I lay my hands on that little bastard…"

"He's dead," I told him. "Dube took him out last night."

"He is lucky I did not get to him first!" Jacob responded with relief in his voice though he tried to make light of it.

We made it to Tigoni and as soon as we passed the police station, my heart started beating fast. What if William was holed in at the house? What were we going to do exactly?

"Perhaps we should wait for Dube," I half – stated and half – asked Otieno and Jacob.

That was what the detective had told us to do. He was assured of backup and we were only the three of us. What if we confronted William and, assuming that he did not kill us, he managed to escape again? The police wouldn't take kindly to that, least of all Dube. But we had to do it – no waiting around.

I asked Jacob to pull in at the Limuru Country Club. If we were going in without police escort, we had better catch William off – guard. Jacob pulled the car into the parking lot of the golf club and we stepped out. Three caddies walked towards us in the hope that we were here for a round of golf but I told them we would be back in a few minutes.

We walked back to the gate and towards the primary school entrance, about fifteen feet from the narrow murram road leading to the Mehta residence. Our best bet was to walk through the school grounds and make it behind the Mehta residence without being detected and then inch our way from behind the garage to the main house.

We walked quietly along a kei – apple fence and once we found an opening, we doubled back towards the back of Mehta's house and soon we were crawling underneath bougainvillea shrubs just behind the garage and inching towards the house.

It was eerily quiet. Even the wind seemed to breeze through the trees silently. I looked at Otieno who was to my right. His forehead was glistening with a little perspiration from the morning heat but his lips still carried that signature smile.

I turned my attention back to the main house. Through the kitchen window, I saw William. He was pacing back and forth and it looked like he was talking on the phone.

"What should we do?" Otieno asked, his voice quivering. "He is alone!"

If Saranya was not already in the house with William, then we needed to let her know to stay away. I pulled out my phone and called her cell phone but there was no answer. I called Dipti.

"Hi Dipti. It's Jack. Jack Chidi. Yes…listen…"

"Hey Jack, why are you whispering?" she asked, alarmed.

"Listen, is Saranya with you?"

"No, why?"

"We are outside her house and…"

"Yeah she should be there by now. I had Anita, my assistant, drop her off early this morning; she said she had to meet some friends. Is she not answering the door?"

"I'll call you back," I said and hung up.

"What now?" Otieno asked.

"I am going in," I answered.

"Just chill out, man, Dube should be here any minute," Otieno tugged at my hand, holding me back.

"Saranya is in there with William," I said. "You two wait for Dube but remember he was going to meet us at the Station."

I crouched and half ran to the kitchen window and listened in. At first I could not make anything out and then I heard the low voices and I pushed my head closer to the window to listen.

"...I know it's been a rough time for you and your mother, but I will always be there for you, you know that," I caught William saying.

"I know. But..." Saranya's voice trailed off.

There was a brief silence and then William said, "I am in trouble and I didn't know who to turn to."

"What kind of trouble?"

"It is absurd. They are after me. They think I killed your father but it's Dave who did it."

"What are you talking about?"

There was more silence and I found myself panicking. After a few minutes I heard him again but I could only catch some words... "I love...come with me..."

I stood up slowly and peered through the window. William was bent over the fridge and Saranya was leaning against the kitchen counter, her arms across her chest.

It was time to act. I tiptoed to the back door and tried it, turning the knob slowly. It opened easily and that's when I noticed that it had been pried open. It must have been how William had got in – he had broken in!

I walked in quietly, leaving the door ajar. I started up the small hallway to the kitchen. I heard him say something to which she laughed. I then heard the sound of heels on hardwood that faded out somewhere inside the house. I stayed put for a few seconds and then I heard water running and assumed that Saranya had gone to take a shower.

Poking my head to the kitchen, I saw William with frying pan in one hand and a carton of eggs in the other. As he turned to walk to the stove, he saw me – our eyes met. He froze in place, his face, a register of fear – but it slowly morphed into a smile.

"Son – of – a bitch!" he said.

I stood up straight and started walking towards him, slowly – my fists clenched. He looked in the direction of the living room and then back at me.

"What is it that you want from me, man?" he asked, trying to sound casual but his face was hardening with anger.

I took one more step towards him and then stopped.

Suddenly, he threw the eggs at me, missing my head by inches – and then the pot. I dove out of the way and rolled behind the kitchen island. Just as I stood up to have a go at him, he pulled out a gun and fired two or three shots – I ducked behind the island again. Then I crawled to the far side of the island.

"Come on, Jack," he invited me. "Let's play!"

I was cornered – no way out and no way to help Saranya – if she needed any help. And then I heard the pitter – patter of feet and I thought he was coming to burrow me out.

"Put your gun down, William!" I heard a voice command.

I peered from the corner. Jerry was the first one to walk in, his rifle ready. He was followed by the OCPD Bernard Lelo, flanked by Agent Njoki and Detective Dube.

Just then, I heard someone run into the kitchen. It was Saranya. William immediately grabbed her and put her in a choke – hold: his left arm around her neck, using her as a human shield. He then placed the gun to the side of her head.

"William! What are you doing?" she asked him.

"Hey, Saranya, it's Jack," I called out from my hiding place. "William killed your father! He lied to you. He is not an oil tycoon! He is nothing but a sex peddler. William, why don't you tell her the truth? Tell her what you really do in Texas!"

"Shut the fuck up!" he shouted angrily. "Y'all back off me now or she gets it!"

"Come on now, just put your gun down and we can all go home." Dube said calmly.

William thought about it for a minute and then shook his head.

"No, I suggest you all put down your weapons and me and the little lady here will walk off and disappear. Poof! Just like that. Or, we can start shooting!"

I crouched to the other corner of the island and peeked out.

"Haven't you done enough killing, William?" I asked.

"For the last time, I did not kill Mehta!" he answered. "I told you, Dave did!"

"But you ordered the hit!" I yelled back, trying to distract him.

"No!" he barked back. "Mehta signed his death warrant the day he threatened to rat us out. And for what – because he found out about me and his daughter here! He was going to expose us and bring down our empire. We had to protect it. The orders came from Agnes, not me. You heard her admit as much. Don't you remember back at the garage?"

With that, he brushed his gun over Saranya's hair, slowly, then cleared his throat and continued.

"But that is of no importance," he said. "What I never did quite understand was why he got so self – righteous about me fucking his daughter – yes, this little sweet thing. Why?"

He was working himself up into a murderous rage.

Saranya had heard enough. She disengaged herself from him and started for the door. William, looking lost, raised his gun towards her. He pulled the trigger. The bullet hit the door, just above her head, shattering the glass to smithereens. Saranya went down, covering her head with her hands.

I heard another shot and saw William's head plop backwards and blood splatter across the wall behind him and then his body collapsed slowly to the kitchen floor.

And just like that it was all over.

Chapter Twenty One

I wrote my story. The Sunday special issue of the *Daily Grind* with William on the cover was snapped up. Other papers, taking a page from our work, ran evening issues with catchy headlines like: *Texan Connection: Sex, Slaves and Murder*, or *Showdown at OK Tigoni*. Others went with more mundane headers: *Global Sex: Sell, Trade or Rent*. It was the international angle that seemed to excite the news editors on print and TV media.

It was a huge story but I did not feel triumphant; I had lost Irene even before we had started and Agnes, head of this cartel was still on the run. All airports in Kenya were on high alert – but she had perhaps made it to any one of Kenya's borders and into some unsuspecting country where she could start a new life.

I called on Dube at his office to thank him.

"There's no telling how deep this shit runs...there is no way they could have operated without help from some internationally well – heeled heavyweights being involved – as investors or beneficiaries. This is Kenya, man. There is much more we have to do before we can say we have touched the bottom of barrel."

"It was the same thing in Texas – they had protection."

He looked at me for a while.

"You are not a bad investigator Jack, perhaps someday you could come and work for me."

"Thanks, Felix, but I think I'll stick with the *Daily Grind*," I replied. "We work best this way, don't you say?"

"Well, I guess so," he admitted. "Anyway, thanks, Jack. Oh, there's one more thing: let me know if Agnes tries to contact you, or if you have any intuition as to where she might be."

"You too, keep me posted on your search," I replied.

He stopped long enough to aim a finger at me, wink and then he let me out of his office.

I called Otieno and then Jacob but neither one answered. I would not have minded a little company but I guessed they needed their rest as much as I did. But I had someone else I needed to see before I was done – Mrs. Mehta whom I hadn't seen since her unconditional release from police custody.

She had started me out on this journey anyway – or rather her husband did. The least I could do was reassure her in person that those responsible for her husband's death were either in custody or dead.

She agreed to meet me for an early lunch at the Tratorria – an Italian eatery downtown.

She had requested a small private room towards the back. I could not tell if she had lost weight or not under the red sari she was wearing but her face looked older, almost haggard. Her eyes had not come back to life but I hoped that I had some news that would bring her a little bit of relief.

"Thank you so much, Mr. Chidi, for coming…"

"Just call me Jack or Chidi…"

She hugged me tightly – her arms trembling for the effort and then invited me to sit down with her.

"You do not know how much this means to me," she started. Her eyes welled up. "Dipti was here but she had to go clear up some paperwork. Saranya excused herself, but that is okay. I wanted to thank you myself." Then she looked right into my eyes. "Thank you so much!"

She put her head in her hands and shook uncontrollably.

I was not sure what to do so I just waited several moments for her to pull herself together.

After a little while, she lifted her head up and dried her eyes. I handed her a tissue I had with me and she blew her nose violently. She then looked for a place to throw the used tissue but there was nowhere, so she tucked it inside her handbag. A waiter came and took our orders; she asked for a roasted veggie antipasto and I asked for scallops and prosciutto bites – had to try something new.

I told her about my visit to Texas, about Agnes, Irene, William and Mohali – the whole works. She listened intently except for the occasional click of her tongue in disgust or disbelief. After I was done, all she could do was shake her head.

Amid sniffles, she managed a whisper: "And to think William was my husband's friend!"

"I guess you really cannot know someone," I offered, looking for the right words in a situation where there are none. She did not say anything more.

The waiter came in with our order, placed it on the table and left. But not before giving me a strange look. It's not every day that an Indian woman dined with an African man in the private booth of a restaurant.

She had barely touched her food by the time I finished my plate. I told her that I had to get back to the office, but if she wanted, I could wait for Dipti to come back for her.

"Oh, no, that is okay. Here, I have something for you."

She reached into a handbag and pulled out a photo and handed it to me – it was one of her husband, Saranya and herself in better days.

"I want you to have it, something to remember us by. I

don't know how I can ever…"

"You don't have to, Mrs. Mehta. I just hope that you and Saranya will find peace after this ordeal. And if you ever need anything, please do not hesitate to call me."

I looked at the photo she had handed me. Saranya was still young but you could see she was coming to herself. She was smiling awkwardly – like most teenagers do when they have to spend more time than necessary with their parents.

"She has turned out to be quite a beautiful woman," I commented.

"Thank you," she answered without expression – her eyes were lost in her pain.

The waiter came back with the check and Mrs. Mehta reached for it. I pulled my wallet out but she was not having any of it.

"No, no! Let me take this," she insisted. "It's the least I can do for all your time and expenses – to say nothing of the risks you took for us."

She handed the smiling waiter a large bill. As we parted, I thanked her again for the lunch. She stood up and gave me a hug.

Chapter Twenty Two

Over the next few days, Dube and his team uncovered a vast network of human trafficking. The underground sex trade was bigger than we had initially imagined. It was an international ring that was supported by several high ranking government officials in Kenya, including an Assistant Minister. Several arrests were made but that was just the tip of the iceberg.

Azani, as part of her plea – bargain, told the Prosecuting Attorney about recruitment offices in India, China, Kosovo and the latest demand for Afghan and Somali girls. She provided names, addresses and phone numbers.

Police raids in posh residences in Nairobi, Mombasa, Lamu and Kisumu, where sex parties were hosted, netted some very influential people and it resulted in the release of hundreds of minors who were being held as sex – slaves.

The information she and Mohali provided helped a well – orchestrated international effort through Interpol to intercept and disrupt some key human – trafficking routes and organizations. For his efforts, Mohali was to get reduced time – a twenty – year prison sentence instead of life.

I had not heard anything conclusive about Irene – I was holding on to hope that her missing person status would change to found and that we could be together. But even that hope itself could not alleviate the gnawing pain that was eating at me.

Dube had called the Houston Police Department on my behalf but they had not located her: she was still a missing person.

Otieno was taking his family upcountry over the weekend and he had asked me to join them. It was a good idea but I was forced to decline – I had to find out what happened to Irene.

I was not sure how I was feeling but I knew I needed a drink, so when Otieno suggested it I was all for it. It was as if he had read my mind.

As soon as we sat down at Anne's Butchery, my phone rang. I answered it with a grumpy hello. After a pause on the other end, I said another hello, more forcefully.

"Hi there, Jack, it's Dale!"

"Hey! What's up, Dale? What's going on?"

"Nothing to it, man. How are you, brother?"

"Still crazy as hell!"

"That's what I like to hear. Hold on man, there's someone who wants to say hi…hold on…here."

"Hi Jack!"

"Irene!"

"How are you?" she asked.

I could tell she was smiling.

"Oh my goodness gracious…what, where…?"

"I'm in Waxahachie with Dale, Gus, and Terry. I'll tell you all about it when I get there."

"You are coming home…?"

The phone cut off and I tried to call back but it sounded busy. Otieno was smiling ear to ear. I guess we both needed good news. My phone rang again and I jumped at it.

"Hi sweetie, I tried to call back." I said.

Silence.

"Hello, can you hear me?" I repeated.

"Hi, there, Mr. Newspaper man."

I felt my body tense up. "You've been quite a lucky boy, wouldn't you say?"

It was Agnes alright.

"What do you want?" I asked venomously.

"Oh, nothing really – you don't think I'll ever forget you, do you?"

Click!

Chapter Twenty Three

At the office I received an email from Irene. She was closing on her house in Texas – her ex – husband had agreed to buy her out. Dale and his friends were helping her with some of the packing. She was going to ship most of her belongings and then fly out in about three to four weeks.

I was elated – finally some really good news! I replied, telling her that I would call her that evening.

I sat back on my chair and placed my feet on my desk. It was not comfortable, so I pulled my feet down and with them came the folder where I had kept all my notes on the Mehta case. I picked it up and opened it, smiling at some Venn diagrams I had doodled on a piece of paper. I reached for a police report Dube had given me that contained Caroline's witness testimony. Just underneath it was a photo of Mehta. If only he had stayed away from William, Mohali and Agnes, he would be very much alive, I thought to myself.

I placed the photo back in the folder and as I was closing it, something caught my eye. It was the photo Mrs. Mehta had given me – the one with the family during happier times. I stared at it for a minute and then focused in on Saranya. She looked beautiful, a huge smile on her face. I then looked at Mrs. Mehta – she looked a little fuller in the cheeks. She wore a gold sari and a lot of jewelry – around her neck, her arms and even along her hairline – but nothing on her face except some heavy makeup. I turned on the desk light and looked more closely. It was then that I saw it.

I called Jerry and told him that I was on the way to see him – I needed to ask for a favor. I grabbed the folder and ran out of the building and took the first *matatu* out to Tigoni.

Jerry was waiting for me outside by the old, dilapidated station building and as soon as we shook hands, he asked how he could be of help. His eyes darted to the main entrance which told me I did not have much of his time.

"I need a small favor."

"Okay, what is it?" Jerry asked, his face softening.

"You said you guys found the knife and also a ring – like a nose ring that Mehta was holding in his right hand, right?"

"Yeah, a small ring, like a clover or some kind of flower. It was covered in his blood. Why?"

"Can I get a photo of it? Please…"

"Well, I don't know. That case is closed now."

"But you still have the files, yes?"

"Yeah, but..."

"Look, I think I am on to something…or perhaps it's nothing. But either way, you will have done me a solid and I…"

"Ok. Let me see what I can do. Let's meet at the Tigoni Stores in about ten minutes."

I did not have to wait long. Jerry had come through for me and he handed me an enhanced photo of the ring. It was a small diamond stud with a flower shaped crown.

"What is this about?" Jerry wanted to know. "It is Mrs. Mehta's ring. She said so herself."

"Did she, really?"

"Positive! But what is this about?"

"I'm just trying to piece it all together for my final report."

I thanked him and left him standing outside the store, puzzled. From there I walked hastily towards Mehta's house. It was not a long walk but it felt like it was taking forever. I tried to control my breathing using a technique my old coach at the university boxing team had tried to teach but it did not seem to help.

At the Mehta house, I rang the doorbell and waited. I could feel my heart beating against my chest. I took deep breath to calm my nerves. I pushed the doorbell two more times.

"Coming!" someone yelled from inside. I heard the locks rustle and then the door opened.

"Hi, Jack! I wasn't expecting to see you," Saranya said as she let me in. "I mean, I did not know you were coming."

"I know I should have called..." I said quickly but she interrupted me.

"Do come in. It's okay. I never did get a chance to thank you."

I followed her to the living room where I sank down on the sofa.

"Can I get you something to drink?" she asked.

"Is your mother here yet?" I asked, impatient to get to what had brought me.

"Yes. Why? What's going on?" Saranya asked. "Why are you looking like that?"

"Could you call her for me, please?"

"She's asleep."

"Go and wake her up!" I said emphatically.

Saranya went upstairs and after a short while, Mrs. Mehta walked down the steps, followed closely by Saranya.

"Hello, Jack. What is it?" Mrs. Mehta asked after they had sat down facing me.

I pulled out the photo she had given me and placed it on the table. I did not say a word but I pointed to the photo.

"You did not have to bring it back, Jack. I wanted you to..."

I reached into the folder again and pulled out the photo Jerry had given me – the enhanced photo of the small nose ring – and placed it side by side with the other one. I heard Mrs. Mehta gasp. Saranya looked at both pictures and then at me – her eyes, wide open, registering shock.

"Oh my God!" she cried and covered her face with her hands – instinctively trying to cover up the small round Band – Aid on her nose.

"I am not sure that I follow…" Mrs. Mehta started but then stopped. The tears now came and she leaned over and fell into her daughter's arms. They both knew the gig was up.

"Mother, please, stop crying! It's all over." Saranya sounded resigned.

"What happened that night?" I asked gently after a few tense moments.

"Jack, please. We have been through enough."

"I need to know the truth – I know about William and your daughter…at first I really thought that William had killed your husband but I am not so sure about that." I said and pointed to the photos. "Not after this!"

Saranya stood up and picked up the photographs and threw them to the floor.

"Saranya! Stop it" her mother admonished.

"No mother! You will not cover up this shit anymore!"

"Hush your mouth!"

"No. Not again! I told you what he was doing to me but you said I was lying. You were always siding with him."

"Saranya, stop it this minute, I tell you! You will just make it worse."

Saranya's tears were now freefalling down her cheeks but she was not crying. Her body trembled but her voice held still. Her mother pulled out a box of tissues and handed one to her. Saranya took it into her hands and slowly folded it into a ball as she re – lived what had happened on that fateful night.

"William had called me to tell me that my father was angry with him, and that he did not want any more contact between us. So when he came home I went to see him in the garage – he was unloading some boxes – parts for his Ford Cortina. He asked me to help open them and place the parts on the work bench. I could not find the box cutter from the tool box so I used a paring knife that was on the side of the box."

She took a deep breath and continued.

"He had asked me if I had seen William lately but I lied and said that he had not come by. He said that he wanted what was best for me and that I should stop seeing the man. I tried to tell him that I loved William but he turned and yelled at me, saying that I was stupid and ungrateful and that I did not know what I was doing.

"I told him that William was good to me and I would continue seeing him. I mentioned that William had promised me a scholarship and work with his oil company if I needed money. My father snapped. His face … he looked different … I don't think I had ever seen him that upset. I said that I wanted to leave … to go and be with Williams or whoever I chose."

"Saranya, please stop it, please …" pleaded Mrs. Mehta. She was trembling uncontrollably.

"No, mother, you need to hear this! He said that he had forbidden me from seeing William. I started to walk away but he grabbed me and threw me to the floor, saying that I was selfish and stupid. I said that he was the one who was selfish and that I would tell everyone what he used to do to me."

"Stop it, Saranya!" her mother continued to plead.

"That's when he threw me on the floor and started to pull my clothes off. I begged him to stop it but he did not. He tore off my bra and started kissing...I tried to push him off but he did not stop, saying that he was going to show me what a real man was like. I screamed for help but he put his hand over my mouth. Then I saw the knife. I grabbed it just as he pulled off my underwear and started to force my knees apart. I closed my eyes and just stabbed him again and again.... The next thing I remember was my mother pulling me away."

"Saranya, I tried to talk to your father..."

"Oh save it, mother! The only thing you cared about was your sham marriage."

"We have customs..."

"Shut up about customs! That's what father said about William and me. And then he would do those things to me... is that Indian custom? And you always kept quiet! What was I supposed to do?"

She now broke down crying and fell to the floor.

Mrs. Mehta got on her knees next to her daughter and held her. She then turned to me.

"Do you have children, Mr. Chidi? Oh yes, yes I remember you said you did not have any, but I hope one day that you will."

She was not being facetious, she was just deeply moved and she was filled with remorse, relief and a whole host of feelings that were tearing her apart – as if she hadn't suffered enough!

Mrs. Mehta was quiet for a minute and then continued.

"At first I did not want to believe it; I was hurt, scared,

angry, shocked and ashamed – all at the same time. So I pretended that it never happened. And I prayed that it would all go away."

She clasped her bony fingers across her daughter's face and massaged her gently.

"When he told me that he was in trouble, I thought he had to pay for his sins. So when I heard the commotion in the garage I knew that they had come for him. I heard someone scream and I ran to Saranya's room – you always run to protect your child before anything else, you know."

She paused as if the irony of her statement had just hit her and then she continued.

"So I ran to her room but she was not there. I then came downstairs, opened the back door and tiptoed to the garage. That's when I saw her, half – naked standing over him with the knife. He was lying on the floor bleeding to death. I could not save him – not after what he had done!"

Mrs. Mehta shook her head from side to side, slowly reliving the horror.

She told me that she helped her daughter clean up and get into bed. She then burned her tattered clothes. After that she walked back to the garage, took the knife and held it firmly in her hands and then placed it next to her husband.

"I am not a bad person, Jack," she confessed. "I just wanted to free my daughter from her misery – to do what was right for her. I was not going to fail her again – I was willing to give up my life for hers. It was the only way I could absolve myself from the pain of *my* silence over the years of abuse."

I waited for her to continue. She took a deep breath and slowly let it out – composing herself.

"It was then that I thought I heard someone – so I looked outside the window I saw him walking away."

"Who?" I asked rather too quickly.

"Dave – I knew he was the one they had sent to take care of him."

That explained the size – four footprints outside the window, I thought to myself. Holy shit!

She stared vacantly into the distance. Her lips quivered but no sound came. I had nothing more to say to her or to Saranya. What could I say? What could anyone say to a daughter who had been regularly raped by her own father? Or to a mother who had stood by and had done nothing?

How was I supposed to write about this? Yet how could I close my ears and my heart to the anguish that both women were suffering? And there was still more to endure now that the floodgates had been opened.

I stood up and walked out.

Printed in the United States
By Bookmasters